Duck, Duck, Truce

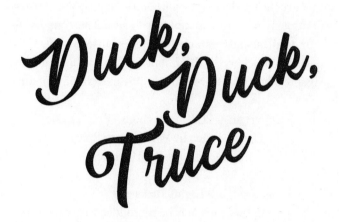

Duck, Duck, Truce

THE LOVE GAME: BOOK EIGHT

ELIZABETH HAYLEY

WATERHOUSE PRESS

To our Boston Besties—Jesse, Chrissie, and Scott: Thanks for taking us to the only bar in Salem that wouldn't serve us...and for riding in the trunk so we didn't have to 😊

Chapter One

OWEN

With all the scientific advancements over the last century, why wasn't time travel a thing?

H.G. Wells wrote about it over a hundred years ago. What the hell were scientists even doing with *their* time?

Wasting it, if you asked me.

Twelve hours. I just needed to go back twelve hours and I wouldn't be an unhappily married man cruising down the highway in an Uber trying to figure out how I was going to tell my ex-girlfriend's family that I'd married her cousin in a drunken depression.

"It's going to be fine, Owen."

"I know," I said so shrilly the driver swerved in surprise.

I cleared my throat before answering Natalia more calmly. "I know. It'll be fine. Vee is totally reasonable. Once we explain, she'll completely understand that I married you so I could be with her. Because why *wouldn't* she understand that? It makes so much sense." My words had somehow grown both more frantic and more sarcastic as I'd spoken.

Natalia reached over and gave my hand a squeeze. "She *will* understand. It's a... What do they call those things in romantic movies?"

"A happy ending?"

"Oh, well, no, that's not what I was thinking. But you'll have one of those too. You'll see."

Will I, Natalia? Will I really?

"It's like a big thing you do for someone to show how much you love them," she explained.

"A grand gesture?"

"Yeah, that's it. A grand gesture. I mean, how much grander can you get than a marriage?"

"Since the marriage didn't include her, I'd think quite a bit grander."

Natalia waved me off. "Such a pessimist."

I'd never been called that in my entire life. I'd never even been much of a realist. But the situation we found ourselves in was dire no matter how much we tried to sugarcoat it. Even my special brand of rose-colored optimism couldn't find a way to shine through this one.

The car pulled into the hotel parking lot, and I began to hyperventilate.

"Owen? Owen! You have *got* to chill out. We'll never get everyone to see the bigger picture if they're busy performing CPR on you."

I dropped my head between my knees to catch my breath.

"Do you need a bag or something?"

I looked up at her. "A bag?"

"To breathe into. Isn't that a thing people do when they're overreacting?"

I straightened up with narrowed eyes. "Are you seriously

telling me I'm overreacting?"

"You're the literal definition of overreacting right now."

"Pretty sure *Merriam-Webster* would disagree."

"Who?"

Jesus Christ.

"Let's just ... get this over with." I shouldered my door open and nearly fell out of the car.

Fuck, I was such a mess. I needed to get it together.

Natalia was right—cooler heads would prevail. I'd just explain what had happened, beg for forgiveness, and it would all be fine. Vee and her family would probably laugh about it. They certainly wouldn't give me cement shoes and drop me in a lake. That was only in movies.

Right?

It was just after ten, and I hoped everyone was still preparing to check out so I could avoid a scene in the lobby, especially since people were likely to notice we were in the same clothes as last night.

I had to talk with Vee. She knew me better than just about anyone. She'd see that my motives had been pure, even if my means had been tainted by Natalia's idiocy.

Not that I could blame it all on Natalia. I'd agreed, after all. Sure, I'd been drunk at the time, but that wasn't an excuse for bad behavior. But that was okay. All problems had solutions. I just had to figure out the right equation for this one.

As I tried to slink toward the elevators, Natalia clomped loudly behind me in her heels.

"Oh, there's my mom. Hi, Mom!" Natalia yelled, causing me to cringe. "She's going to be impressed I married a guy with a job, even if it is a marriage of convenience."

"Is it convenient?"

"Well, yeah. It's convenient I was there to get you into the family so Vee wouldn't have to worry about that anymore."

"You do understand that if I'm married to you, I can't ever marry her, right?"

She laughed. "We're obviously not going to stay married. Once we've proved our point, we can get divorced."

I didn't even know what point we were trying to make anymore. Last night, when Natalia had said we'd show Vee her concerns about me being part of her family were silly by getting married ourselves, I hadn't questioned her logic. Vee couldn't object to me becoming part of something I'd already joined. But in the light of day, the cracks in that reasoning showed clearly. Vee was going to be pissed.

"My mom's waving us over. Come on." Natalia started to walk away, and I quickly reached out and gently took hold of her arm.

"Natalia, wait. Seriously, you have to see how messed up this is. Everyone is going to freak out and very possibly hate me, which is the exact opposite of what I was trying to make happen."

Natalia sighed heavily. "Yes, okay? I see how this was not the best idea I've ever had, but we can't take it back, Owen. The only thing to do now is own it and double down. You can't expect Vee to see the good in your intentions if *you* don't even see them. We're gonna need to just . . . fake it till we make it."

"What are we making exactly?"

She looped her arm through mine and smiled. "A mess. But, man, is it gonna be an epic one."

VERONICA

I woke up this morning with puffy eyes and a headache. I almost texted Owen after listening to June's voicemail but felt it was better to talk in person. But after the way I'd acted, I figured a little space might be good for both of us. The next time I spoke to Owen, I wanted to be sure of my words. He didn't deserve someone jerking him around.

When I got up, I realized Nattie wasn't in the room. Her bed was still made, and her suitcase hadn't moved from where it had been the night before. I wondered if she'd noticed I was upset and decided to give me space, but she'd never been very observant, so that seemed like a stretch.

I shot her a text to check in and then headed to the bathroom to shower and try to get myself together. After I was done and no longer looked like I'd been on a bender, I checked my phone to see if she'd replied.

We're all downstairs.

I wondered what "all" meant but figured I might as well just find out for myself. Especially since I wanted to scope out the continental breakfast anyway.

When the elevator doors opened to the lobby, I stepped out into chaos. Members of my family were all gathered around Nattie and Owen.

What the hell is happening?

I walked over toward the group, picking up snippets of the conversation as I went.

"Natalia Rose, you tell me right this second where you've

been," my aunt Ana sniped.

"Don't middle name me. That hasn't worked since middle school."

Ana narrowed her gaze, and Nattie physically recoiled.

"Okay, fine, it still works. We took a little road trip."

"Where?" my uncle Chris, Ana's husband, asked.

Nattie mumbled her response, prompting Chris to say, "Where?" more forcefully.

"Connecticut," she practically yelled.

"What the hell were you doing in Connecticut?" Manny asked.

"And why weren't we invited?" Franco added.

"I told you, we just wanted to take a little road trip," Nattie said.

While the rest of my family debated the merits of impromptu road tripping, I wove through the crowd until I was next to Owen.

"Hey," I whispered in his ear.

He jumped before whipping his head toward me. "Vee! Hi. Wow, the whole family's here now, huh?" He looked how I imagined a cornered owl on speed might—all big eyes and jittery disposition.

"Can we talk?"

"Talk?" His voice broke on the word as if he'd hit puberty this morning. "About what?" he asked.

He was being super weird, and it put me on high alert. On one hand, he could've been overcompensating for last night's drama by trying—and failing—to be overly chill this morning. On the other hand, he'd fled to Connecticut with my cousin. I didn't want to think anything had happened between them, but why else would he be behaving so oddly?

"About last night."

"Last night?" He cast a panicked look in Nattie's direction, which made dread coil in my belly.

God, had *he slept with her?* Owen wouldn't do that to me . . . would he?

"Yeah. You know . . . our fight?"

"Oh, that!" he said much too loudly. "Yes, uh-huh, I'd like to talk about that. Maybe over there, and away from . . . here." He pointed toward a seating area at the far end of the lobby.

"Sure," I replied warily before I started in the direction he'd indicated.

"Wait! Where are you two going?" my uncle Ricky asked.

"I need to talk to Owen," I said. "Privately."

"Not until I find out what he did to my daughter," Chris said.

"Easy, Chris," Ana cajoled as she patted his arm. "Pretty sure protecting Natalia's virtue is a day late, dollar short kinda thing."

"I just want to know what they were up to all night," Chris said, looking a little green at the implication of Nattie's sex life.

I turned to look at Owen. "What *were* you doing with Nattie last night?"

"Last night? With Nattie? Uh, why do you think we were doing something?"

Tears prickled my eyes. I *needed* to know what had happened because something clearly had. I knew the fight was my fault, but him running off with my cousin definitely wasn't. And fuck Nattie too for that matter. What kind of family member skipped the state with your boyfriend on a whim?

I took a deep breath, willing my voice to stay even. "Owen, I need an honest answer. What did you and Natalia do last night?"

"We just took a drive," Nattie cut in.

"Neither of your cars left the parking lot," Frannie said.

She turned to glare at him. "We'd had a bit to drink so we took an Uber, *Dad.*"

Frannie scoffed. "If I were your dad, I'd hook myself to an IV of vodka every day. No offense, Uncle Chris."

Chris waved him off.

"So you wanted to go for a drive, but you took an Uber? Does that make sense to anyone?" Manny asked.

"It doesn't have to make sense to you," Natalia argued.

"But it does need to make sense to me," Uncle Ricky stated, his voice clearly indicating he was tired of playing games.

"Owen," I said, my voice close to pleading.

"It needs to make sense to me too," Chris added. "Just tell us what you were doing. Did you get arrested or something?"

Man, how I hoped they said they were arrested. That was much preferable than the X-rated possibilities.

"Owen," I said again.

He looked from me to my family and then back to me, and I almost felt bad about how scared he looked. But then I remembered that he wouldn't need to be scared if he hadn't done anything wrong, and my resolve hardened.

"Maybe we should go up to one of the rooms," Natalia said. "This isn't a great place for a conversation."

"No, you'll tell us right now," Ricky demanded.

Squabbling broke out. We were definitely causing a scene, but I didn't take my eyes off Owen. He looked so lost, and I hated that my first instinct was to comfort him.

The voices around us grew louder, and Owen and I seemed to have a whole conversation with only our eyes.

Please, my eyes begged.

I'm afraid you won't understand, he seemed to say back.

Realizing I wasn't getting any answers from him, I turned to Natalia. Three steps brought me into her space, causing her to jerk back as if I'd slapped her.

I lifted a finger so it hovered in her face. "So this is how it is, huh? I've always been in your corner, but the first chance you get to stab me in the back, you take it?"

"Vee, listen, it's not like that."

"Then what's it like? Tell the truth for once in your pathetic life."

Her eyes widened and then narrowed to slits. "Excuse me? Who the hell do you think you are?"

"I'm the person who's about to kick your ass."

"Oh, please. You wouldn't risk breaking a nail, golden child."

My family moved between us as we continued to hurl insults at each other. If I had gotten my hands on her, I would have throttled her.

The commotion we were causing reached a point where I wouldn't be surprised if the police were called. Jesus, never mind my family not being good for Owen. I was as crazy as they were. But I couldn't pull my temper back. It was like a wildfire had erupted within me, and it was so consuming, Smokey Bear himself wouldn't have been able to extinguish it.

I tried to get to Natalia as she yelled at me, and our family yelled at us both. Then suddenly, a voice rang out from behind me.

"We got married!"

Time seemed to stop as we all fell quiet and slowly turned to stare at Owen.

"What did you just say?" my uncle Ricky asked.

Owen's eyes held nothing but apologies, but I couldn't accept any of them as he repeated himself. "We got married. Last night. In Connecticut."

And then all hell broke loose again.

Chapter Two

OWEN

To say the drive home was tense would've been an understatement.

The air in the truck felt so thick, it was like trying to breathe through quicksand. But no matter how much I wanted to make things better, there was no getting out of this one. So I'd stopped trying to explain. I figured the best course of action at this point was no course of action. That line of thinking led to a painfully quiet ride home, but quiet was preferable to the alternative.

Figuring she'd let her brothers drive her back, or that she'd decide not to go back at all, I was surprised when Vee said she'd still drive home with me.

It physically pained me to think about how much I'd hurt her, and I was going to have to bear the weight of that. But once we started driving, my torment became so much worse.

When I turned on the radio, Vee put in her headphones so she didn't have to listen to the same song as me. When I tried to make the temperature in my truck as comfortable as possible for her by messing excessively with the air conditioning controls and vents, Vee opened her window and let the air whip against her face and hair as she stared out. And when I'd pulled into a rest stop and grabbed us some drinks and snacks, Vee had said a simple, "No thanks."

She played on her phone, listened to her own music, sipped on an iced tea she'd brought with her, and practically ignored my presence completely. I thought about asking her if she'd rather drive and have me ride in the bed of the truck so she didn't have to share the same air as me, but I was scared she might take me up on it, so I kept the offer to myself.

I was actually surprised I was even capable of driving. I'd thought for sure that her brothers would kill me when I'd said I'd married Natalia. I think they'd intended to, but Vee's running off and my running after her had likely been what had saved me. Even though Vee had barricaded herself in her room and refused to answer me—or let Natalia in—I'd stationed myself outside her door.

Natalia had filled in the rest of the family about our drunken mistake, and everyone had taken some time to cool off before they decided what they were going to do about it.

I wanted to ask her what they'd do but thought ignorance was my better option for now.

Finally, Vee emerged, declaring she was driving back with me, and that was the last we'd say about it. I'd completely destroyed all the headway I'd made with Vee's family. Not to mention everything I'd destroyed between her and me.

When we finally arrived at the house, Vee hopped out of the truck, grabbed her bag from the back seat, and walked toward the house without a word. It all felt strange as fuck, and it was all my fault.

Well, my and Natalia's fault, but that small detail hadn't made the situation any better.

"Let me know if you need a hand," I called to her as she headed up the steps.

Without turning around, she raised the arm that wasn't carrying her bag and flipped me the middle finger without slowing her pace.

"Guess that's a no," I said to myself.

Sighing heavily, I hung my head. It had become my standard posture since I'd realized I'd tied the knot.

"Fuck," I said louder. Then I grabbed my own bag out of the back seat and slammed the door to my truck. This living situation was gonna be about as fun as filing my toenails with a chainsaw.

Over the next few hours, we managed to avoid each other fairly easily. I did some laundry while Vee unpacked and did whatever other shit she did in her room that didn't involve me.

When she finally emerged after an hour or so and came downstairs, I perked up like a Labrador whose owner had just walked in the door. Maybe she'd pay attention to me or talk to me or simply look my way.

I raised my eyes from the book I'd been trying to read to take my mind off my shitshow of a life that involved sharing a house with my ex-girlfriend while I fantasized about my divorce from her cousin.

Vee passed by me without acknowledging my existence in any way. She opened the fridge and pulled out some lunch meat to make herself a sandwich, and I thought about how it would probably be a while before I had any type of appetite.

And this was our routine for the next few days, passing by each other silently, eating alone, coming and going without sharing anything about our day with the other. It felt like I was living with a ghost of the person Vee had formerly been. Or maybe *I* was the ghost, like in *The Sixth Sense* when Bruce Willis walked around for the entire movie thinking his wife was mad at him only to find out at the end that he'd died in the beginning.

And man, could I relate to poor Bruce, because at least a part of me died the night of Vee's grandfather's party. And then just for good measure, like the fuckup I was, I'd gone ahead and squashed any small chance I had of ever getting her back.

That was a fact I'd have to accept, even though the veracity of it made my heart feel like it was shattering all over again. This was my new reality, and if I wanted to survive it, I'd have to adapt. It wasn't exactly what Darwin had envisioned when he'd created his theory, but the same premise still applied here.

But as much as it hurt to think that Vee and I could never be what we'd been, what was even worse was thinking that I'd lost her as a friend. And maybe—eventually—our friendship would be something I could salvage.

That thought brought me back to all the texts I'd avoided since coming home. Carter had reached out a few times to see how the trip had gone, and when I didn't text back, he asked if he should tell the police to start looking in the Hudson River for my body.

Nah, I'm alive. Just been busy.

It was all I could manage to write back because while I wasn't in the mood to talk about the weekend, I'd accidentally thrown away the best thing that ever happened to me. Avoiding his texts would only lead to his curiosity piquing.

But by day six with Vee in my house but not in my life, I couldn't take it anymore. I needed to know what she thought. About me, about *us*. I needed to know what her plan was. Did she want to move out, or did she just plan to pretend I didn't exist until the fall semester was finished? It was sad that I'd happily be ignored if it meant she'd stay in the house with me. But not knowing was killing me.

So as she entered the kitchen where I was sitting eating a bagel with Gimli—my own little Haley Joel Osment—beside me waiting for some fallen crumbs, I said abruptly, "How much do you hate me?"

It wasn't what I'd planned to say, and you'd think after almost a week of playing out every version of this conversation, I would've come up with something better, but it was what it was.

She finished pouring her coffee, put in a splash of cream and a teaspoon of sugar, and mixed it thoroughly before she even bothered to set her eyes on me. When she hadn't responded right away, I thought for sure she wasn't going to respond at all. So it surprised me when she did. And there wasn't a word in the English language that could adequately convey my complete and utter shock when she said, "I don't *hate* you."

"You don't?" I tried to keep my voice steady, but I heard the uncertainty in it. Though she'd said the words, their meaning was hard to believe. How could she not hate me when I hated myself so damn much?

"No." Vee still hadn't looked at me, but I didn't need to see her eyes to know she was hurting. "I did at first. Or I thought I did. But the more I thought about it—the more I tried to digest what you did, the more I realized the feeling I attached to your actions was more disgust than hate."

Well, shit. "I'm so sorry, Vee."

She sighed heavily, holding the mug tightly between her palms like the warmth provided the comfort she so desperately needed. "Yeah," she said with a sad shake of her head. "You've said that so much to me that it's lost its meaning."

"But I *am* sorry. And I don't know what else to say to make things between us better." I wished I could reach out and hug her, close the physical and emotional distance between us and never ever let her go. But she wasn't mine to hold on to. And she probably never would be.

The sound that came out of her mouth at my apology sounded as close to a laugh as I'd heard from her in a week. Only there was no humor in this one. Only anger and sadness and probably a whole host of other negative emotions she'd associate with me from now on.

"There's nothing you can say—Christ, there's nothing you can *do* to make this better. It's not like you canceled a date, Owen. You fucking married my cousin."

"I did that *for* you, though. I did it for us. I love you, and when you broke up with me, I was devastated."

"Okay, so we're really gonna do this? You wanna talk about this, let's talk." She was stern, confident, so sure of herself without compromising her composure even during such an emotional conversation. She was gonna make one hell of a lawyer one day. "Let's start with the fact that when someone breaks up with you, you get them flowers. Or you give them space. You don't marry their fucking relative."

"I know. I was drunk and—"

"Drinking's not an excuse for a decision like the one you made. Would that have been your excuse for cheating on me too? 'I was drunk'?"

"I'd never cheat on you," I said softly, hoping she'd hear the sincerity in it, see the truth in my eyes. I could tell Vee was about to cut me off again, and though I couldn't blame her for not wanting to hear anything I had to say, I needed to try. I'd opened the door to this conversation, and I need to walk the fuck through it. "I know you don't want to picture me in your family. I get that. I really, really do. After what happened to your mom, I understand why you're afraid."

"You don't understand anything about why I'm afraid or what I'm afraid *of*. You couldn't possibly. Your grandparents are alive. Your parents are alive. Hell, they're still married, which is pretty much unheard of today. You had a nice, southern upbringing probably full of chicken soup and 'atta boys' when you brought home anything higher than a C on your report card."

Her voice began to grow louder as she spoke, but it sounded more frustrated than angry. Whether the frustration was with my lack of understanding, my idealistic childhood, or me altogether, I wasn't sure.

But she continued. And eventually her frustration had simmered below the surface for so long that when she turned up the heat, all of it boiled over.

"So don't stand here and fucking tell me how heartbroken you were when you'd thought you lost me. You," she bit out sharply, "know absolutely nothing about loss."

I waited until I knew she was finished. The last thing I wanted to do was interrupt her. It gave me time to collect my thoughts and consider what I'd say before I actually spoke.

"You're right," I finally admitted quietly. I didn't think it was possible for me to feel more splayed open than I had this past week, but Vee's accusation proved I was wrong about that as well. "I don't have a lot of experience with loss. And certainly nothing that compares to what it felt like to lose you. I was unprepared and didn't know how to react, so I panicked."

Rolling her eyes, she shook her head at me. "Panic? Jesus, Owen, I know you love being this free-spirited impulsive guy who everyone loves, but I don't," she said, her expression hardening to match her words. "I don't love you anymore, and it was obviously a mistake to let myself *ever* fall in love with you."

Was that true? Had I fucked up so epically she couldn't possibly love me anymore, or had she simply said that in the hopes that hearing the words out loud would cause the idea to manifest?

I wanted to argue that love wasn't something she could just turn off. If she'd ever felt it, the remnants of it should still echo somewhere within her. But maybe that was wishful thinking, and who was I to lecture her about it anyway? I'd already acted like she should take job advice from me. Me: a twenty-three-year-old kid who was experiencing his first truly life-changing event. Vee had endured more as a child than I had up to this point.

I was such an asshole.

"I understand," was all I could manage as a reply, because even though it hurt, it was true.

I was a blip on what would be the timeline of Vee's life—something she'd recall with just enough detail to tell her own children about mistakes and poor decisions. I'd be a life lesson—a foggy memory of one of the many obstacles she'd had to overcome to get to wherever she'd end up in life, which no doubt would be somewhere without me.

The realization saddened me more—terrified me, even.

But not as much as thinking that maybe, after enough time, I'd be nothing to her at all.

VERONICA

"What do you mean you understand?" I finally asked after a beat of silence.

I wished I could've had more than six days to have this talk with Owen so I could get my thoughts in better order, but it was what it was. I couldn't avoid it forever, despite desperately wanting to.

My initial reaction to Owen's confession had been avoidance, but I was due some answers. I hadn't been ready to hear it at the hotel or in the car ride home. It was all I could do to pretend like what he'd done hadn't destroyed me. The ride back had been me proving to myself that I could face difficult things. It was time to prove that again, even if that meant confronting some hard truths about my role in all of this, as well as what I knew about who Owen was.

Maybe after I'd broken up with him, he'd felt so betrayed that he'd married Natalia to hurt me—to show me I no longer had an influence on his decisions or his life. But that rationale didn't seem very Owen. He could be reckless and clueless and sometimes completely oblivious. But one thing he wasn't was vengeful.

He cast his eyes toward the ground, a gesture that showed me how ashamed he felt. But he managed to look me in the eye before he spoke.

"I get why you don't love me and why you probably never will again."

I chose not to point out that I hadn't used the word *probably* and let him continue.

Shrugging, he added, "But that doesn't stop me from loving you."

"Don't do this."

"Do what?" He seemed genuinely confused, probably more so since the comment had come as a response to a question *I* had asked.

"Talk about love. This isn't about love." I tried to sound firm because I knew Owen well enough to guess that he wouldn't accept that as an answer.

"Isn't it?" He took a step closer to me, though it was so subtle I almost hadn't noticed it. I wondered if it had even been a conscious movement on his part. "Because to me that's exactly what this is about."

"What love? Your love for Natalia?" I spat, causing him to jerk back like I'd punched him square in the face.

"You know I don't love Natalia. That's ridiculous. I'd only known her a few hours."

"Yet you eloped with her." The words sounded silly, but my tone was anything but. I'd done well so far keeping it together, bottling up all emotions except anger and frustration because I refused to show any feelings that could be seen as a weakness. "How did you think that would make me feel? Huh? Did you think about any of that? You couldn't have."

I would *not* cry in front of Owen. I wouldn't even cry in private *about* him. I'd promised myself. But there I was, standing in front of him, struggling to blink back tears I knew would fall if I didn't get out of this situation. Yet I couldn't stop myself from engaging in a conversation that would result in my inevitable collapse because the walls I'd built around myself were made of cards. And I knew Owen could knock them down with so much as a glance.

"No," he said. "I didn't think anything through at all, and I'm so sorry for it. I know you don't want to hear that, but I am. I'm an idiot who tried to find a solution to a problem that I hadn't identified all the variables for yet."

When he stepped closer, I put a hand up to stop him. "Don't come near me. Please," I said more quietly.

He stopped completely and then walked farther away to the kitchen table and took a seat. Fidgeting with a pen that had been sitting there, he said, "I know I fucked up, and I'd do anything to take it back. But I can't. So all we can do is figure out how to move on from here."

At least he was right about something.

"I'd be selfish to try to convince you to take me back, so I won't. And more than that, I don't deserve your forgiveness."

"Well, that's good because you're never going to get it." I tried to sound certain, sure of myself. But the more I looked at Owen sulking sadly in front of me, the more doubtful I became of my ability to hold my ground. And I hated myself for it.

"So where do we go from here?" Owen asked. "Are you planning to find another place to live, or . . .?"

"I haven't decided yet." It was the truth. If I got an apartment, I'd have to pay for it, which obviously wasn't preferable from a financial standpoint. But from a mental and emotional one, I wasn't sure how I could continue living with Owen. Plus, for some reason, it made me feel guilty to stay here if we were barely on speaking terms. But then, I wasn't the one who'd gone and fucked up our relationship. At least not in a way that was so permanent.

My mind felt like the wheel of a stationary bike turning

rapidly without making any forward progress. I absolutely should *not* feel any sort of responsibility in this. Yet I did.

"You don't have to find somewhere else to live," he said. "Having you pay for a place when there's a room here you've already settled into would make me feel like a bigger asshole than I already do."

"We wouldn't want that, would we?"

"That's not what I meant," he said, backtracking when he'd realized how his comment could be interpreted. "I just meant—"

"I know what you meant," I replied, my voice noticeably softer than it had been a moment ago. My body slackened more than it had since we'd come home, as if I'd finally released some of the tension. I couldn't feel this angry forever. I couldn't even feel like it for a solid week.

At some point, especially if I were entertaining continuing to live with him, I'd have to figure out how to share a space with him. I'd have to learn how to breathe the same air as him and sleep under a roof he slept under even though I'd never sleep in the same bed.

"I'll take the next few days to decide for sure if I'm staying or going. Is that okay?" I asked, because when it came down to it, the house was still Owen's.

"Yeah." He perked up at my reply, but he seemed to temper his expression. "Of course. Take whatever time you need to figure things out or find another place if that's what you decide. I'll do my best to stay out of your way." He was probably caught somewhere between not wanting to seem too excited and not wanting to let himself *become* too excited—too hopeful. "You can pretend I'm not even here."

"Honestly?" I said. "That's what I've been doing since we

left the hotel. Turns out I'm pretty shitty at pretending."

"Or maybe I'm just really annoying." His lips turned up into a smile that didn't quite form fully.

I almost laughed. "That too," I agreed, trying to sound as dry as possible.

He stared at me for a moment that felt longer than it probably was. I did my best not to maintain eye contact. But despite how painful it was for both of us to lock eyes with the other—how it felt like digging into wounds that hadn't begun to heal—neither of us looked away.

Owen rubbed a hand over the scruff he'd grown on his face and sniffed. It was the type of sniffle that would come from someone who either just snorted a line or someone who was trying to hold back a well of tears. And since Owen hadn't developed a coke habit that I knew of, I had to believe he was more bruised than I realized. I'd been so focused on my anger and feeling like a victim of someone else's stupid decision, I hadn't considered that Owen was a victim of his own stupidity too.

Not that I actually gave a shit.

"So is this like a truce?" Owen asked. "At least a temporary one?"

"I don't know if I'd call it a truce. It's more of an agreement, I guess. No fighting or being passive aggressive. Just kind of a temporary break from how we've been around each other the past week." As I explained, I realized how dumb that sounded because I'd pretty much given the definition of a truce. I almost expected Owen to call me on it, but he seemed to know better. "So yeah, for lack of a more fitting word, we'll call it a truce."

"Sounds good." Owen nodded before standing and extending a hand to me. When I didn't take it, he muttered,

"Too soon. I get it." Then he put his hands in his pockets and exited the kitchen like we hadn't just agreed to the impossible.

Chapter Three

VERONICA

Owen and I had been doing some kind of depressed game of hide-and-seek where we intentionally *didn't* look for the other. I knew the logical thing was to find somewhere else to stay—there was no way we could go on like we were. But part of me didn't want to make things easier on him. Let him have to share a space with the person he'd betrayed. Served him right.

But as time passed, I had to acknowledge that part of me didn't want to leave because then it would truly be over. I wasn't completely unreasonable. Despite what I'd said to him when we'd argued, I knew people made mistakes. And while his had been pretty shitty, I could maybe get over it. Eventually.

Only time would tell, but if I left, I'd be stopping the clock on our relationship forever. Because while some might think getting some space from each other would do us good, I knew myself better than that. If I left, I'd use the distance to put up a wall I'd never be able to knock down. I'd turn into June—having what I wanted blocks away but being too damn stubborn and worried about what other people thought to go get it.

My family had offered to help me pay for somewhere else. They were obviously less than thrilled with Owen—or Natalia, for that matter—but had thankfully deferred to me. But if I left Owen, they'd celebrate it, and then it would be awkward if I took him back. Would they think I was weak? That I was blind to reality? That I'd let a man run all over my feelings without consequence?

And what if Owen moved on after I left? Beyond running off and getting married to my cousin. *Bastard.*

Owen wasn't home—he probably had to work—so I had the house to myself. It sucked that things were so tense because I truly loved Minnie's house. Since I'd been helping renovate it, it truly felt like home for me. Losing that would suck almost as much as losing Owen.

God, I was a total mess. One second, I was railing at him about how I'd never forgive him, and the next I was convincing myself not to leave. Emotions were the fucking worst.

As I went into the kitchen to get a snack, my phone vibrated in the back pocket of my jeans. The display showed it was my uncle Ricky, and I was tempted not to answer. My family meant well, but they'd been checking up on me like I was one nasty word away from being sent to the loony bin. But Uncle Ricky tended to overreact, so I wouldn't have put it past him to find someone to send over here to check on me if I didn't pick up.

"Hi, Uncle Ricky."

"Hey, Vee. How ya doing?" he said in a tone one might use when checking in on someone newly widowed.

"Fine," I said. Fine—the word people who were decidedly *not* fine always used to describe themselves. "Things are going well," I added in an attempt to be more convincing.

"Yeah?" Ricky replied, sounding doubtful. "How's that guy you're living with?"

I couldn't help but be amused. My whole family had been enamored with Owen, and now he was reduced to *that guy*. No one could ever accuse my family of not supporting their own.

"He's fine." *Damn it!* "Busy with work and fixing up the house."

"He's not bothering you, is he?"

"No, he's been good about giving me space."

"Cause I can send him a message if he's not. You just say the word."

"That's . . . definitely unnecessary. Thank you, though."

"Yeah, well, the offer stands. Anyway, about why I called. I think it's about time we cleaned up this mess with Natalia and that joker down there. I made some calls and found someone who can help them get annulment proceedings started."

Annulment. I obviously knew what the word meant, but I hadn't considered it because I hadn't thought there would be grounds for one. But if Ricky knew someone who thought they could make it happen, then maybe their sham of a marriage wouldn't follow us like some kind of nuptially challenged albatross. An annulment would basically erase it. And if the law treated it as if it had never happened . . . maybe I could eventually do the same.

"You think an annulment is possible?" I asked, trying to keep hope from seeping into my voice.

Ricky snorted. "Money makes all kinds of things possible. Owen and Natalia will have to go back up to Connecticut to meet with the guy I found. I'll give you his number, and you can all work out the details."

He gave me the contact information, and I wrote it down.

After telling him I'd keep him updated, we said our goodbyes.

I sat at the kitchen table staring at the phone number in my hand, wondering—and hoping—that this would be the answer we needed so we could all start moving on. Whether Owen and I moved on together or apart, well, that was still anyone's guess.

OWEN

When Mark had called and asked if I'd wanted to pick up an extra shift, I jumped at the chance to get out of the house. I hated that this was what Vee and I had come to, but here we were. Even though it was Natalia I'd married, Vee and I were acting like a disgruntled couple on the brink of divorce.

The bell jingled above the door, signaling the arrival of a new customer, and I plastered a smile on my face as I rounded a corner to greet whoever was there. The smile slipped when I saw Vee standing there, looking pensive.

"Hey. You okay?" I asked as I rushed forward.

She gave me a small smile, as if she found my concern cute. Or maybe I was just reading into it.

"Yeah, I'm fine," she said. "Uh, do you have a second to talk?"

I nodded. "I haven't taken my break yet. Let me tell Mark I'm stepping out."

I didn't wait for a reply before turning and heading to the back to find Mark, who sent me off with a wave and a request to bring him back a coffee from the café down the block. The man had a serious caffeine addiction.

"Ready," I said when I rejoined Vee, and I held the door

open for her as we stepped into the afternoon sunshine. "I promised Mark a coffee, so do you mind if we head to the Bean?"

"That's fine." She didn't say more, so I figured she wanted to wait until we were settled to tell me what she'd come to say.

I hoped this wasn't a *you'd better sit down* kind of conversation. What if she told me she was moving out? Even though I probably should've expected something like that, I couldn't bring myself to. It would be so . . . final. I had to believe I could still fix things, even if all signals pointed toward the opposite being true.

We went into the Bean and ordered before sitting down.

"So what's up?" I asked, unable to wait any longer.

"Ricky called."

I shifted on my seat, anxiety creeping in. Was this the part where she told me he wanted to have me fitted for cement shoes?

She opened her mouth to continue, but our names were called by the barista.

"I'll get it," I said. When I returned with our drinks, I looked at her expectantly.

"He said he knows someone who could help with an annulment. It'll involve you and Natalia going back up to Connecticut to meet with him, but"—she shrugged—"it could be a good option."

There was something about her ambivalence that seemed forced. I hoped that was because she was still invested enough to want my marriage with Natalia to be dissolved.

"It sounds like a great option. Thank you."

"I didn't do anything. It was all Ricky."

I didn't know what to say to that, so I took a sip of my drink.

We sat there in silence, and even though that had become the norm for us, I still felt the unbearable strain of it in every part of my body.

"I can't promise this will fix anything," she blurted out. She darted her eyes to make brief contact with mine before looking back at the cup in her hands. "Between us, I mean. Though I guess I can't promise it'll fix the mess with Nattie either. It's just a meeting. Who knows what will happen? But with us, I don't... I can't... Jesus, I'm rambling." She took a deep breath before continuing. "I can't help how I feel."

"Of course not," I assured her.

"But part of me feels silly for feeling that way because I know you didn't do it to hurt me. I realize drunk logic isn't sound logic. But it hurt me anyway, and I just... I don't know how I'll feel with time or with an annulment or... anything."

"I'm not asking you for anything, Vee. Not because I don't want something, but because I have no right to expect it."

She nodded. "Maybe we can take it a day at a time?" she said. "I'm tired of being mad, but I can't go back to how things were either. So maybe we just do what feels right in the moment? See if we can at least rebuild a friendship?"

I smiled. "I'd like that."

She offered me a small smile in response. "Okay. Good."

Things weren't fixed by any means, but it was as if a tiny sliver of the shattered mass that was our relationship had been glued back together. Hopefully we could keep rebuilding, piece by piece, until we at least somewhat resembled what we'd been.

Chapter Four

OWEN

I didn't know what made me agree to meet the Scooby Gang at Ransom and Taylor's apartment complex for a summer cookout.

"I'm not a good liar," I told Vee as we walked from the parking lot to the courtyard entrance where the pool and grills were located. We'd driven separately but figured it would invite more questions from our friends if we didn't arrive together. "They'll find out the truth eventually, so let's just tell them now. It'll be less awkward."

I held the gate for Vee to enter, and she cast a look my way like I should be ashamed I'd even suggested such a thing.

"Oookay, so that's a no to coming clean."

We hadn't spoken about what happened since the night we'd agreed to a truce, and clearly there was a good reason for it. If we couldn't discuss it with each other, we couldn't tell our friends.

"I know we can't keep it a secret forever," she admitted as we walked up the stone path to where our friends had set up.

"But this is mortifying for me." The words gritted through her teeth like she was afraid if her lips moved, someone might read them. "My boyfriend got married . . . *is* married to my cousin."

"It's mortifying for me too," I told her. "Maybe even more so because it was my dumb mistake."

"Don't even make this about you right now."

"I'm not trying to. I'm just saying that it's not like it's gonna make me look good. Everyone's gonna feel so bad for you and think I'm the reckless dumbass who caused all this."

We'd been walking at a pretty quick clip, but Vee stopped abruptly and turned to face me. "Did it ever occur to you that I don't *want* anyone to feel bad for me? I don't need people's pity."

"Sympathy isn't pity, Vee. There's nothing wrong with your friends supporting you through a difficult time. Maybe it'll help to talk to some of the girls." I shrugged casually. "Brody and Ransom have done all kinds of stupid shit."

"Oh. Did they marry random people too?"

"Okay, point taken," I told her. "Not a great comparison, but I hope you know what I'm trying to say." Hoping Vee saw the sincerity in my eyes, I willed myself to convey with my body language what apparently my words couldn't. I was like the opposite of King Midas—everything I touched seemed to turn to complete shit, and I was so sorry for it. "I just . . ."

I wasn't quite sure how I'd planned to finish that sentence, so I was thankful when a voice from a distance yelled, "Yo, O, you guys comin' up here, or you planning to have a romantic dinner by the pool?"

I looked away from Vee to see Carter standing on a short stone wall with his hands around his mouth like he was calling into a megaphone.

"I'll bring the food to you as long as you give me a good tip," he said.

Not wanting the group to say anything else regarding romance and the two of us, we both continued the rest of the journey up the brick path. If this were *The Wizard of Oz*, I obviously would've been the Scarecrow. Though I'm pretty sure Vee could make a damn good case that I didn't have a heart either.

"Just . . . don't say anything about anything one way or the other," Vee reminded me in case I had any doubt about which topics were off-limits tonight. "If they ask us about the trip, which I'm sure they will, let me lead the discussion."

"I don't like lying, though," I said, not because I was trying to make the situation more difficult but because I genuinely sucked at it. Plus, I liked when people knew who I was, what I thought. I didn't want to hide any part of myself from these people any more than I wanted to hide myself from Vee. "I'm really bad at it, so this makes me nervous."

"I'm sorry, but I can't worry about your feelings right now," she said quietly, "but if you can't say anything that's a lie, then don't say anything at all."

"I don't think that's how the saying goes."

"Aamee already volunteered to help me hide your body if death should come to collect you early."

My eyes widened at that. "Are you being serious?" And because I knew she probably was, I followed with, "Why would she say that?"

I thought I saw the side of Vee's lips turn up into a smirk that didn't quite form entirely. "Don't feel special. She offered it to all the girls."

"Oh," was all I had a chance to reply with before we made

it to our friends. And despite the fact that everyone seemed happy to see us—even Vee looked like she wasn't looking quite as . . . grim as she'd been since we'd returned home—I had a feeling this was gonna be a really long night.

VERONICA

It was tougher than I thought to try to act normal around Owen and our friends. I'd been so worried about the truth spewing from him like cheap alcohol out of a reckless teenager that I found myself unable to focus on anything else.

Then there was the other side of the coin—the one where we had to pretend we were still together without actually *acting* like we were still together. The last thing I wanted was Owen getting too close to me or touching me or . . .

My eyes drifted over to where he was sitting on the edge of a chaise longue, his legs wide as he rested his forearms on his thighs and held a beer. He appeared so at ease—calm even despite obvious tension.

I hated him for it. If I didn't know better, I'd think he didn't give a shit about everything that had transpired over the last couple of weeks. But I knew he gave a shit. Even though there was no do-over, no mulligan to rectify marrying Natalia, I knew he wished he hadn't done it.

Yet somehow he was able to smile while he held a conversation with Ransom and Taylor. I even saw him laugh once or twice. He was either a fantastic actor—which I doubted—or he would get past all this faster than I would.

And then there was me, sipping on a Twisted Tea like it was my only friend. I desperately wanted to talk to someone but simultaneously be left alone.

So far I'd managed to get by with little conversation, which I appreciated. I'd expected everyone to flock to us like we were celebrities who'd come back from the dead since we'd both basically gone off the grid for the past couple of weeks. Maybe they could sense something wasn't right between the two of us. Or maybe they just didn't give a fuck about our relationship as long as we still showed up to hang out.

"Anyone up for a game of LCR?" Brody held up the small tin of dice and shook it excitedly.

Aamee groaned so dramatically, her whole body seemed to participate. "He's been obsessed with this game lately," she said before hanging her head and flopping her long blond hair over her face.

"I'll play," I said, thankful to have a distraction.

"It sucks," Aamee said. "Could you not infer that from my initial reaction?"

That made me laugh a little, and Aamee reluctantly got up when I did to head over to the table.

"Don't listen to her," Brody said. "She just hates playing when it's just the two of us."

"How do you start a game with two people?" Drew asked, sounding genuinely curious. "There's no left or right. That's two-thirds of the game."

"I just pretend there's a third. I set up an empty chair and give the imaginary person chips and everything," Brody explained, like the answer should be obvious.

"That's pathetic," Sophia said to her brother.

"*You're* pathetic," Brody shot back, but as always, there didn't seem to be any malice behind it.

"Good one," Sophia said. "We're playing for money, right?

Because I plan to take all of yours."

"Well, I barely have any, so joke's on you."

Sophia rolled her eyes and turned to Aamee. "Remind me what you see in him."

Despite her previous teasing of Brody, Aamee stood at his side and looked up at him adoringly. "He's fun and sweet, and he makes me laugh."

"Thanks, babe," Brody said with a broad smile.

"Laughing *at* him doesn't count," Sophia pointed out.

Aamee continued to rattle off some more of her boyfriend's appealing qualities, including being competitive and not taking life too seriously.

He kissed her in between compliments in a way that was somehow both cute and revolting.

"Are we gonna play or not?" Carter asked before chugging the rest of his beer and putting the red cup down hard on the table. "Wait, actually, anyone up for beer pong? I feel like I'd rather play a game that takes some athletic skill."

Beer pong wasn't exactly athletic, but none of us pointed it out to him.

"I'm in," I said, liking the idea of standing and moving around rather than sitting at a table next to or possibly across from Owen.

"Fine," Brody said. "It's been a while since I played, and the last time we filled the cups with bong water. Most of us got too sick to finish the tournament. I've actually been wanting to play ever since. With beer this time, of course."

Like most of Brody's comments, we ignored that one. The rest of the group agreed to play, and the guys set up the table and pulled the chairs away.

"So how are we doing this?" Drew asked. "My vote is

tournament-style with a losers' bracket."

"No losers' bracket," Ransom said. "If you don't win, you shouldn't be in."

"Okay," Drew said. "Fair enough."

We agreed to put in ten bucks each, and the winner would get the full pot.

"How do we decide the teams?" Sophia said.

"Teams? We can play individually," I suggested.

"No way. We don't have a shot against most of the guys. Carter and Owen have been in a frat, Ransom played professional football, and I'm pretty sure Brody has played beer pong more than he's showered over the last few years."

"Hey," Drew said, sounding offended. "What about me?"

Sophia looked him up and down. "I have no knowledge of your beer pong skills, so it would be unfair to make an assessment. I actually wish Xander were here so I could be his partner. He probably has an algorithm or something for this."

"Maybe Xander wouldn't want to be *your* partner," Drew offered. "I don't have any knowledge of your beer pong skills either."

Sophia shrugged. "I suck. That's why I need a good partner."

"Let's just do couples," Aamee said. "It's the easiest way."

"But what about Toby and me?" Carter said. "We don't have anyone . . ." He looked around to all of us, but Toby took hold of his arm and pulled him close against him.

"Yes," he said. "You do." Then he smiled at Carter sweetly.

The rest of us were silent, but I had a feeling I wasn't the only one thinking *It's about fucking time.*

The two guys stared at each other for a moment that felt full of everything I'd recently lost before Carter said, "What are you . . . what are you talking about?" His voice was quiet, unsure. Like he didn't want to make assumptions that could lead to his own disappointment but couldn't help but hope anyway. "You don't have to do this if you're not—"

"Stop talking," Toby said, putting a finger over Carter's lips to silence him. Then Toby breathed deeply, closed his eyes for a moment, and interlaced his fingers with Carter's. "Carter and I," he said, looking back to Carter. "We . . . we're . . . I haven't been ready to tell anyone. It's been killing Carter for I don't know how long. And now it's killing me too." Gone was the initial hesitation in his voice. It had somehow been replaced with a confidence even Toby seemed surprised he'd found. "I can't pretend anymore, Carter. I can't pretend I don't love you when I love you so damn much."

I watched Carter inflate with something so beautiful, my emotional wreck of a self couldn't even identify it. "I love you too," Carter said. "So much. You know that."

They pressed their foreheads together, and Toby nodded against him. "I know," he said. "And now everyone else knows too."

They brought their lips together for a brief moment before turning back to us.

"You guys make a good beer pong team," Owen said with a smile. "I think I speak for all of us when I say I'm glad you stopped pretending."

"And also," Aamee said, "you both suck at pretending, so I think for all of our sakes, I'm glad we don't have to keep pretending either."

"You knew?" Toby's eyes widened.

"Of course we knew," Drew said with a smile. "It's not difficult to see when people like each other. You two look at each other like crushes on an elementary school playground."

Carter put his arm around Toby's shoulder and squeezed. "Told you we should've just admitted this months ago."

"Why didn't you?" I asked. I wondered if we were the first people they shared their relationship with or if they'd told their families but found it difficult to tell their friends. "I mean, if you don't mind me asking."

They had to know that our group would accept them—be *happy* for them.

"Honestly?" Toby said. "It was my hesitation about all of it. Growing up, I didn't exactly make friends easily. I wasn't athletic or social like Carter. I guess I was so used to being judged that I didn't want to relive that feeling."

I caught a glimpse of Owen, his sandy hair flopping into his face before he pushed it out of the way. He looked genuinely confused.

"You think any of us would judge you?" he asked, glancing around at our group.

"I should've known better, I guess," Toby said with a sigh.

"Damn right," Ransom told him, his voice holding a sternness that was probably meant to convey how much we all loved Toby. "You're stuck with us whether you like it or not. Remember when no one knew I was a stripper?"

"That's not the same at all," Taylor told him.

"I'm not comparing stripping to sexual orientation. I'm not that dense. I just mean it's hard to keep any secret with this group. I don't mean that they'll find out—though they will. I'm talking about what it does to you inside when you keep something to yourself that you feel is too huge to share."

"Like when Drew pretended he was me and it looked like Sophia was fucking her brother," Brody said with a slow nod.

"Nope," Sophia said. "Not like that. Probably more like how you felt when you had to pretend you were married to Vee."

That wiped the smirk off Brody's face quickly.

Aamee rolled her eyes at the memory. "Am I the only one who hasn't had something to hide around here? Jeez."

"Owen hasn't," Carter said. "He's clean as a baby's ass after a diaper change. My man's an open book."

My eyes darted to Owen, who not only reddened at the comment but also seemed saddened by it.

His sky-blue eyes found mine for a moment before he looked away again. I imagined the connection, as subtle and short as it was, might have been too painful for him. Just like I knew how painful keeping such an embarrassing secret probably was for him. He wasn't the guy who hid things. He was too pure, too honest. Which was exactly why I'd been so scared about him becoming wrapped up in my family.

Owen gave Carter a small smile that faded so quickly I was surprised he'd managed it for any length of time.

Even though I knew he wanted so badly to come clean about his mistake, I knew he never would because I'd asked him not to. He'd already hurt me enough.

But I'd also hurt *him* enough, and it was time to stop punishing both of us.

"Owen married my cousin Natalia while we were away," I said.

Chapter Five

OWEN

What the hell?

At first I thought I heard Vee wrong. Or maybe I just wished I had, because as much as I hated being dishonest, now that the feral cat was out of the flimsy paper sack we'd kept it in, I realized I hated people knowing I'd married someone else even more. It wasn't that I felt like a fucking idiot—though there was that too—it was that I'd done something so incredibly thoughtless and inconsiderate.

Clearly, neither of us knew what to say after Vee's bombshell, because we both remained silent. Even our friends were speechless, though that was short-lived, and I wished I'd thought to enjoy the quiet a little more, because what came after the silence ended was a barrage of questions ranging from, "You're kidding?" to "Is she hot?" to "Do you have a death wish?"

I found myself unable to speak for an awkwardly long time. Though, the entire situation was awkward as fuck, so I wondered if anyone even noticed. When I finally found my voice somewhere deep inside me, I chose to ignore the stupid questions and focus on the ones that mattered. The ones that could possibly do something—anything—to begin to repair my relationship with Vee, even if it was just to maintain a genuine friendship.

My heart quickened as I tried to maintain composure. It was important to me that I didn't appear frantic, because then it would seem like I hadn't reflected on my mistake as much as I should have. Especially when all I'd done since the morning I'd woken up married was think about what I'd done and how I wished I could change it. But the purpose of reflecting was to make sense of a situation and ensure history didn't repeat itself.

Though, since there was no way in hell I'd ever let myself marry my girlfriend's relative again, reflection did nothing except make me feel like a bigger piece of shit. If that was even possible. If Apple made a new poop emoji, they might as well use a picture of my face.

"All right," I said, as calmly as I could. "I know what I did is unforgivable. I do. Believe me. I can't forgive myself for it, so I would never expect Vee to."

I looked over to her as I said it, and I wondered if she'd immediately regretted telling everyone what happened. I also wondered why she'd done it in the first place since she'd been so adamant that I keep my mouth shut about it. But none of that mattered now.

"Hold on," Sophia said, waving everyone off as they continued to fire questions my way. "Let's just let him start at the beginning. How did this all happen? Take us through the weekend."

"Okay." I sighed, feeling slightly light-headed but still

feeling the need to stand as I shared what happened. I did my best to recount the trip to them—our drive up, finding out Vee and I wouldn't be sharing a hotel room, meeting Natalia. "Vee and Natalia aren't really close."

"Oh, good," Aamee said. "So you didn't just marry any cousin. You married one Vee doesn't really like."

"You're not helping," Sophia snapped, giving Aamee a stern stare.

"Well, *nothing* can help a fuckup this major, so . . ."

"So you're just gonna make it worse?"

Aamee rolled her eyes but didn't say anything else.

I continued. I told them how I'd gone to the girls' hotel room with Franco and Manny so we could all walk down to dinner together, how the meal had gone as well as I could've hoped for.

"So what'd you do?" Brody asked. "Celebrate by proposing to her cousin?"

"Jesus Christ, you two are truly meant for each other, aren't you? You've really mastered the art of inappropriately timed comments."

I was surprised the comment had come from Vee because it momentarily felt like we were on the same side of this debacle. Or more accurately, that she wasn't *opposing* me.

"Thanks," Brody said, smiling at his fiancée. But then he turned to me and said, "Sorry, bro. Bad joke. I'm just trying to make you guys laugh."

A few of our friends laughed at that, though it seemed like they knew they probably shouldn't have.

I didn't know if Brody's comment was supposed to make me feel better. If it was, it missed its mark. Especially because that *someone else* was Vee. I knew he was just trying to be

Brody—lighten the mood and make me see the humor in all of this. And I hoped maybe one day I would. That day just wasn't today.

"If everything was okay, I don't get it," Ransom said. "How did you end up marrying Vee's cousin?"

My eyes darted to Vee, who dropped her gaze to the ground before speaking. "We got into an argument."

We did? I wouldn't have considered it an argument, but I didn't want to correct her either.

"About what?" Drew asked, probably because no argument he could think of would cause him to basically elope with one of Sophia's relatives.

I saw Vee's mouth open a bit, though she looked unsure about whether she wanted to speak.

"Doesn't matter," I said. "But instead of going back to the dinner, I stayed at the bar and tried to forget what had happened between us. Eventually Natalia saw me." I hated having to retell this moment almost as much as I hated the actual memory of it. If I'd been sober, this wouldn't have happened. If I'd gone up to the room before everyone finished dinner, this wouldn't have happened. If I'd done anything but share the intimate details of my conversation with Vee with Natalia, this wouldn't have happened. "She asked what was wrong, and I told her. Then we drank more, and she suggested we get married." I sighed. "You know the rest."

"Oh, so *she* proposed to *you*," Brody pointed out. In response to the glares from all of us, he said, "Sorry. Again."

I looked around at our friends. They seemed to be digesting all of what I'd just told them. I wondered if anyone would say anything of value that could possibly help. I highly doubted it. I'd said more than enough, so I waited for someone else to speak.

Finally, someone obliged. "I get that you had too much to drink, so obviously your judgment was skewed at the time, but I don't get why you guys thought getting married would help your situation with Vee."

I knew someone would eventually ask this because I'd left out the circumstances of our breakup. I learned my lesson having shared them with Natalia. I didn't think it was my place to tell anyone else about the specifics.

Looking at Vee, I wondered if she'd speak up. When she did, I was both surprised and relieved. She told them the truth about her fear of me getting too close to her family, how she didn't want it to corrupt me or mar me in some way.

"You act like he's a naïve toddler," Carter said. "This is the same dude who whacked it in front of his grandmother."

Vee didn't even get a chance to respond before I said, "I didn't 'whack it' in front of her." He'd made it sound like I'd done it intentionally. The last person I wanted in my fantasies was my Grandma Jimi. "She walked in on me. I bet some of you have similar stories."

Everyone looked around at each other for a few seconds before there was a murmur of, "Nope" and "Not really."

"You know what I mean," Carter said. "Owen's a big boy. If he wants to live a life of crime, who are we to stop him?"

By *we*, I assumed he meant Vee, and he didn't want to call her out. At least that was what I hoped he meant, because it meant that at least one of our friends could see the situation from my perspective.

"It's okay," I said. "I understand why Vee freaked out. She has a right to feel however she feels. I overreacted and made a rash decision that fucked everything up. When Natalia said getting married would mean I was already in the family, I guess

45

it sounded like an idea that might work. To my intoxicated brain anyway," I said with a heavy sigh.

"Doesn't seem like the *worst* idea," Carter said. "It feels like you were just panicking and throwing shit at a wall to see which piece stuck."

Toby cocked his head at Carter. "I don't think that's the phrase. Throwing shit at a wall. Like actual pieces of shit?"

"Yes, actual pieces of shit, Toby. Picture it. Makes perfect sense. You take a pile of shit and toss it at a wall. Some sticks and some doesn't."

I actually found his logic difficult to argue with.

"Whose shit are we throwing in this scenario?" Toby asked. "Because I wouldn't want to touch my own, and I sure as hell wouldn't want to touch someone else's."

Carter stared at him for a moment before shaking his head and saying, "It's a metaphor."

"If I can interject for a moment," Vee said, "I don't think marriage is something you toss out to *see if it sticks*. Marriage always sticks because by the very definition, you're forever legally connected to the person."

"Not forever," Aamee said. "I know a great divorce lawyer." She'd already taken out her cell phone and was scrolling through what I assumed were her contacts.

"Jesus Christ," Vee muttered. "I shouldn't have brought this up. But you guys were talking about secrets, and . . ." There was a sadness behind her eyes. "I just felt like we should come clean about why we've been ghosting everyone since we got back. No point pretending we're together when we're not."

The way she looked at me made the sadness come back to my eyes too, and I found myself hoping I would look away without being able to actually do so.

"Well, thanks for telling all of us," Toby said. "You don't have to talk about it anymore if you don't want to, but you know if you need our help, we'll be here for you."

"Thanks," I said with a nod, and Vee smiled.

I wondered if she was relieved that she'd told our friends what happened or completely regretful. But much like the marriage, there wasn't anything that could be done about it now. Maybe now we could move on and hang out as friends.

Or maybe now I'd have to be close to the woman I loved without ever being close to her the way I wanted to be.

Chapter Six

VERONICA

Thankfully, for the rest of the night, Owen and I had somehow found a way to get back to normal. Whatever our normal currently looked like, that was. We still stayed as partners for beer pong, and much like the trivia game, Owen dominated most of the games we played. We made it to the final round where we faced Toby and Carter. Turned out they made an even better beer pong team than they did a couple.

We hung out awhile longer after the round ended, and it was good to be with our friends again. As much as I thought I didn't want everyone to know what had happened between Owen and me at my grandfather's birthday weekend, it felt surprisingly freeing to be honest with them. Maybe it would make it easier to move on from my relationship with Owen now that we'd officially *un*-coupled.

By the time we made it home, I felt like we'd both gotten to a place that would be manageable for both of us.

"What are your thoughts about tonight?" I asked as I looked in the refrigerator for the white Gatorade. For some reason, it seemed easier not to face him.

"As far as what?" Owen grabbed a glass from the cabinet and set it on the counter.

I thanked him and smiled. "As far as being honest about you and Natalia."

He shrugged and then grabbed a red paper clip that was lying on the counter and began pulling it apart into a different shape. "It surprised me, that's for sure. But you know I hate having to hide anything, especially from people I care about, so even though it makes me look like an asshole, I'm glad they know." He looked up from the paper clip. "Thank you."

I nodded slowly before putting the Gatorade away. Why did he always have to be so polite? It would make things easier if he could just act like the jerk I'd thought of him as recently. But with every nice gesture and kind word, I found my will to dislike him evaporating like a puddle on a hot day.

"I've been thinking . . ." I said. "About whether to stay here or find a new place."

His eyes widened as he looked at me. I couldn't tell if he was excited or nervous about what I had to say. Probably a little of both.

"And?"

My lips twisted a little before I spoke. "And it's probably easier if I just continue to stay here. I don't want to have to move all my stuff again and find a new place. It'll probably be difficult to find anything decent for a price I can afford right now because the semester's about to start. I'm sure anything I'd be interested in is already taken."

Owen nodded like my justification made sense. It did to me too.

"If things aren't going smoothly, I'll reevaluate in a few months."

"Great. Yeah, sounds like a good plan." Looking relieved, he gave me a small smile. One that didn't show his dimples but let me know he was happy. We'd continue living together, and we'd no longer have to dodge our friends or pretend to be something we weren't. "I guess I'm gonna head up to bed then. See you in the morning?"

"Yeah." I smiled too, but it was quick.

He grabbed a bottle of water from the case by the basement stairs before heading toward the front of the house to go up for the night. Stopping at the bottom of the stairs, he looked back at me.

"Thanks again." He didn't wait for me to reply before jogging up the stairs with a lightness he'd been missing since we'd come back from New York.

OWEN

Vee had just come back from a run with Gimli when I finally decided to get out of bed and make some coffee before I began my weekend project—replacing the back door. There was a gap at the bottom that let air in. I'd considered putting weather stripping at the bottom instead of replacing the whole thing, but the wood was banged up anyway, and it had never quite closed correctly, so I figured I might as well replace the whole thing instead of putting a bandage on the wound.

"Did you ever go down that gravel street off Highland Drive?" she asked, letting Gimli off his leash.

He greeted me briefly and then headed to his favorite spot on the living room couch while Vee grabbed a bottle of water and twisted off the cap.

"No, I don't think so. I don't think I know what street you're even talking about."

She took a long drink. "Probably because it looks like a driveway until you go down it. I only noticed because I wasn't driving. In a car, you'd probably go right past it."

"What's down there?"

"About five or six houses and this cute little farm. They had two horses and a few goats that I saw. They must have chickens too because they had a little sign that said they sold fresh eggs."

"Oh, cool," I said, unsure of exactly how I was expected to respond. I had no idea why she was telling me this, but I was certainly glad she was choosing to talk to me.

"Maybe we should get some chickens. We could sell eggs too. Eventually maybe we could get a cow and have, like, a dairy farm here. There's enough land for it."

Had she gotten a brain transplant since I'd last seen her? "Um, I don't know if we're ready for that. I have my work cut out for me just trying to fix what needs attention. I don't think I'll have time to tend to a bunch of farm animals. And you start school in a few weeks. I'm not sure farm life suits us right now."

She thought for a moment as she gazed out the kitchen window into the large yard. "Yeah, you're probably right," she said. "I figured maybe we could make some extra money that way, but I'm sure it's a lot of work, and it probably costs more than I'm realizing to have animals like that, so it's a wash anyway."

"Why is this the first I'm hearing about your love of barnyard animals?"

She laughed before looking back at me. "I wouldn't say it's a love of *barnyard* animals specifically. I've always loved animals. We had all kinds growing up. One time Franco and Manny brought home a ferret some girl was giving away at school, and my mom let them keep it. They fought over naming it for a few days before they finally settled on Diane because it was the first name of their ninth-grade homeroom teacher who they swore the ferret resembled."

Vee paused to smile at the memory before continuing. "Sometimes they'd let it roam the house, and our cat would chase it. Eventually they became good friends though and would sleep together in my bed at night."

My eyes narrowed and my jaw parted slightly as I tried to determine which aspect of her story to focus on first. Finally, I settled on the beginning. "Can we back up to why someone brought a ferret to school?"

She shrugged. "Beats me. People are weird."

I couldn't argue with that. "I wish I'd known you slept with a ferret when I was worrying about how you might feel about living with Psycho Joe over there." I nodded to where Gimli was standing with all fours on the coffee table so he could see out the window to the backyard.

"Well, if we're being technical, Diane slept with *me*."

I laughed out loud at that. "I guess if you can befriend a ferret, having a couple of chickens or something around doesn't seem too weird."

Vee looked at me and sighed heavily. "Honestly, nothing seems weird anymore."

And wasn't that the fucking truth?

Vee turned back to look out the window. "I have to tell you something," she said. Her quiet, sullen tone made me instantly tense.

"Yeah?"

"That night…at my grandpop's party?" When I didn't respond, she went on. "June called that night. Left me a message."

The mention of June made my heart rate speed up. We'd put so much effort into finding June and getting answers from her about Minnie, it had been anticlimactic when we'd actually met her. Elements of June's story hadn't added up, but I'd given up on getting closure about who Minnie had really been. Maybe some things were meant to remain a mystery.

"She said she lied," Vee continued, finally turning to face me again. "She and her husband and Minnie were lovers. But rumors started spreading, it hurt their business, and they had to make a choice. According to June, they chose wrong. She said she regrets abandoning Minnie. That she always loved her."

Her voice sounded like she was reciting times tables— emotionless and factual.

I knew why she hadn't told me. I'd imploded our worlds hours after she'd probably listened to the voicemail.

"Thank you for telling me," I said, unsure of what else to say.

"I always meant to. Things just got…crazy. But Minnie was your friend, and you had a right to know sooner than now. I'm sorry for keeping it from you."

"You had your reasons."

She shrugged. "Doesn't make it right."

And that was the crux of it, wasn't it? We'd had reasons for so many things, but having a reason didn't make something right.

"I still have the voicemail. You can listen to it whenever you want."

"Thanks. I'd like that. But . . . not yet. For some reason, I don't feel ready to hear it yet." There was no way I wanted to hear about someone losing a love of their life and all the pain that loss caused. That was too close to home at the moment.

"Sure. Whenever you're ready," she said, and I was thankful she didn't push me to listen or ask why I wanted more time. "I'm gonna go shower."

"Okay," I replied as I watched her walk out of the kitchen, Gimli hot on her heels.

At least one man in this house was welcome to follow. I just wished it had been me.

Chapter Seven

OWEN

When Vee's uncle Ricky had said he knew someone who could help us get an annulment, I hadn't expected that person to be an actual judge.

After I spoke to Natalia and we agreed on a day that worked, I called the number Ricky had given. A man answered, but he didn't identify himself as a judge. All he did was gruffly tell me he knew the situation and gave me an address for where to meet him. Which ended up being a courthouse.

Thankfully we were in his office and not an actual courtroom because I wasn't sure I could handle having to get up on a stand or anything official like that. Not that I even knew that kind of thing was done in annulment cases, but I was still thankful, just in case.

Natalia and I squirmed in the large black leather seats that sat across from Judge Kline, who appraised us gravely from behind a giant desk. When he huffed and sat forward, I assumed he'd found us lacking.

"Mr. Diaz contacted me about you two needing an

annulment. I assume you've both read up on the requirements for such a thing?"

Natalia and I shared a bewildered look. I was suddenly thankful Vee had decided not to come with me. If she saw I hadn't even done the most basic preparation for this meeting, she'd definitely never forgive me. Naïvely, I'd assumed someone would walk us through the intricacies, but evidently we were being thrown into the deep end without a life jacket.

When it didn't look like Natalia was going to speak up, I replied, "Uh, I didn't, um, know we were supposed to." My voice rose at the end as if the statement were a question, and I realized I sounded like a complete idiot. Which would maybe work to my advantage if the judge decided I was too stupid to consent to a marriage.

He let out a deep breath and said, "Just as well. You don't qualify for one anyway."

The feeling of your heart dropping to the floor? Yeah, turned out that was a real thing. I'd never experienced it before, but when he told us we couldn't get an annulment, that was exactly what happened.

His words caused Natalia to find hers. "But my uncle said you could help us." She sounded on the verge of a complete drama-queen meltdown, and I wondered if I should try to get her out of here before we were held in contempt or something. Getting arrested would not cause the Diazes to warm back up to me.

The judge stared at us again, and I had to admit, it was unnerving. This guy was probably hell on criminals. I'd have confessed to whatever he wanted if it meant he'd say something.

"You don't qualify, but there are . . . allowances that can be made."

Oh, shit. Was this where he said one of us would have to be his sex slave in order for him to grant us what we wanted? Because I was willing to take one for the team—*anything for you, Vee*—but I didn't want to put Natalia in that position.

Natalia and I shared another glance before turning our expectant gazes on the judge.

He steepled his hands and rested them over his mouth like some kind of cartoon villain. "Mr. Diaz made a comment that stayed with me." He paused for so long after that sentence, I wondered if we were supposed to guess what Ricky had said. Finally, he continued. "Seems he's tired of cleaning up your messes," he said, directing his attention at Natalia. "And I'm tired of reckless, entitled young people relying on other people to solve all their problems. So I'm not going to grant you an annulment."

That heart-dropping thing happened again.

"Yet," he added, and my chest gave a hopeful flutter. "You want to make adult decisions rashly? You can suffer the consequences. Maybe that'll teach you a lesson."

I wanted to argue that I'd already learned a lesson when I'd lost the most important person in my life . . . but thought better of it.

"I'm not following," Natalia said. "I thought you told my uncle you'd help us?"

The judge shrugged. "Who's to say what will help you the most?"

Natalia scoffed. "I feel like *I'd* know what would help me most."

The judge looked interested, but in that patronizing way of people who thought they knew everything. Funny how he'd called us entitled, but he was the one who acted like holding our futures hostage was some kind of right he deserved.

"Do you now?" he asked. "Tell me, whose idea was it to get married?"

Natalia's jaw ticked before she said, "Mine."

"And what was the reason you suggested it?"

She looked at me for a second, her eyes full of what looked like regret. "I thought it would help with an issue Owen had."

"And did it?" the judge asked, his gaze finding mine.

"No," I said quietly, not wanting to lie but also not wanting to announce how bad of a decision it had been. On both our parts.

Looking back at Natalia, he said, "So it would appear you actually *don't* know what will help a given situation."

Natalia looked down at her hands, fisted on her lap.

I felt bad for her. Granted, her idea had been terrible, but I'd gone along with it. We'd been drunk, but we obviously hadn't been that far gone. We'd managed to get ourselves to Connecticut and convince someone to marry us, so we'd had to have at least seemed reasonably lucid.

I didn't have many memories of that night, but I knew a lot of that was due to how resolutely I'd refused to think about it. The hangover from hell I'd woken up with the next morning had made me a little slow on the uptake, but I hadn't been too wasted to make the right decision that night. I'd chosen not to.

I was as culpable as Natalia, even though part of me had wanted to lay the blame primarily at her feet. If I wanted to fix things, maybe that started with taking more responsibility.

"She wasn't the only one who made bad decisions that night. We both made mistakes, but we'd like the chance to set what we can right again," I said.

"Oh, I'm aware you're no choir boy yourself," the judge said to me.

I wanted to inform him that I actually *had* been a choir boy when my grandma had gone through a brief Evangelical phase when I was eight but decided it wouldn't really be helpful.

He continued. "The only way to learn from mistakes is to suffer the consequences of them."

"Sir," I said. "With all due respect, I think forcing us to remain married is a pretty steep consequence."

"I'm not forcing you to do anything. You can file for divorce anytime you'd like."

He was right. We could, and it would likely be easier than dealing with this insufferable man. But Vee had seemed... relieved by the prospect of an annulment. Like that night could be erased if we went this route. Even if it weren't true, maybe she could convince herself to give me another chance if the marriage never happened, at least on paper.

"But if we want the annulment?" I prodded, wanting him to just get to the point already.

"Then you're going to give marriage a go." When I opened my mouth to argue, he held up a hand and continued. "For three months. For three months, you will live together and experience what it's like to be in a marriage. Then maybe next time, you won't rush into one."

My mouth opened and closed like a gaping fish. What he was suggesting was insane. First off, Natalia and I didn't even live in the same state, so how would we move in together? Secondly, even if she did move in, we'd basically be roommates. How would that teach us anything about marriage?

But before I could organize my thoughts enough to voice them, the judge held up a hand. "Save it. You acted like you'd do whatever it took. This is what it takes. Accept my offer or get the hell out of my office."

Part of me wanted to be mutinous. Wanted to storm out of there with my middle finger waving. But the part that wanted Vee back kept me in my seat, even though I slouched back against it like a defeated man.

I turned to Natalia. "What do ya say?"

One corner of her lips tipped up in a grim smile. "Your place or mine, hubby?"

VERONICA

"What the hell do you mean Natalia is moving in?" I screeched into the phone.

I'd told Owen to call me as soon as he was done with his meeting, but I was wishing I'd had him wait until he was home. For whatever reason, I felt like I'd have understood what he was saying more easily if I'd been able to look at him. And yelling would have been much more satisfying if I could've seen his reaction.

"That was the judge's stipulation," Owen explained. "Well, one of them."

"What are the others?" I asked through gritted teeth.

Owen sighed. "Marriage counseling. And he wants us to do things together and take pictures or videos to prove we're doing them."

"What kinds of things?"

Owen hesitated. "Couple-y things. He wasn't very specific. But he wants proof that Natalia and I are spending time together. He wants us to try to make the marriage work."

I'd never understood the phrase *seeing red* before, but suddenly, I got it. "Why would he want you to try to make a marriage work that he's going to dissolve in three months anyway?" My throat tightened as something dawned on me. "Is he hoping you won't go through with the annulment?"

I rubbed at my chest, hoping to ease the ache there at the prospect of Owen deciding he wanted to stay with Natalia.

"I actually don't think so," Owen replied.

I remained silent so as not to reveal how relieved I was to hear that.

"Honestly, I think he wants to make us suffer. He wants us to have to jump through so many hoops that we never make a mistake like this again."

"He thinks marriage is a mistake?" Who the hell was this judge Ricky had found? He sounded like a real dickhead.

"No, not, like, the institution of marriage. But our marriage, yeah, for sure. He also thinks we're spoiled brats who've had everything handed to us. So I guess he wants to make us work for it."

"Well, he read Nattie pretty well, then," I muttered like the salty bitch I'd become. "So she really has to move in here?" I asked again, hoping I'd somehow misunderstood everything Owen had said since the call began. "Can't she just come down, take some pictures, and go back home?"

"I don't think that'll work. First of all because I think your uncle really wants us to suffer, and he may rat us out if we're not meeting the requirements. Second, we had to promise, and you know how I am with lying."

"Yeah, yeah, I know," I muttered.

"I'm—I know I've said this a thousand times, but I'm sorry, Vee. Truly."

I was silent for a minute, trying to figure out how to reply. I finally settled on, "I know that too," because I did know. I just hadn't gotten around to fully accepting the apology yet. But I would. Hopefully. Though having Nattie around twenty-four seven probably wouldn't really help me get there.

I'd only ever enjoyed her company in small doses. And that had been *before* she'd married my boyfriend.

"Uh, there's one more thing," Owen said, the hesitance in his voice making me tense.

"What?" I whined because seriously? When would it be enough?

"We need to, uh . . ." He sighed.

"Spit it out, Owen."

"I need to take Natalia to meet my parents before the three months are up."

Parents I hadn't even met yet. Right. Awesome.

I groaned and rubbed a hand over my face. "Let's just . . . table that for a couple of weeks. Okay?"

"Yeah," he agreed easily, probably relieved to put that shitshow of a meeting on the back burner for a bit. "Okay."

Chapter Eight

VERONICA

Grumpiness had become a constant state for me since Owen had told me about his meeting with Judge Kline. I did my best to hide it and thought I was mostly successful, but I felt it constantly.

And as Owen and I sat around waiting for Natalia to show up, I worried that I'd never get over it.

I loved my cousin. I truly did. But I was pissed, and having to live with her for the next few months was going to suck. There was no silver lining that I could see. Just a constant need to practice restraint so that I didn't murder her. I doubted Judge Kline would be willing to help get me out of that one. Not that his brand of helping was super effective anyway.

"She's here," Owen said, breaking me out of my thoughts.

I sighed heavily before standing begrudgingly and making my way to the front door.

Natalia was already out of the car, pulling her things from the back seat as her brother Adrien unloaded the trunk. Owen jogged to help them as I ambled slowly behind.

Nattie eyed me warily as I approached. Maybe she wasn't as dumb as I'd assumed.

"Hey," she said.

"Hey."

She looked around for a second, her eyes darting anywhere but to me. Finally she added, "Guess we're going to be roomies." She tried to infuse excitement into her voice, but it came out sounding strained.

"Guess so." And okay, maybe I could've made more of an effort, but I hadn't clawed her eyes out upon her arrival, so she'd have to take that for what it was worth.

We hadn't spoken since the wedding debacle. She'd tried to reach out, but I'd ignored her. Owen had made all the arrangements for her arrival and kept me abreast on a need-to-know basis.

There'd been very little I'd needed—or wanted—to know.

"This place is . . . cute," she said in a tone that let me know that wasn't what she truly thought of the place.

Well, screw her. If she didn't like it, she could find another place to live. Like a cardboard box on skid row perhaps.

"Vee and I have been fixing it up bit by bit," Owen said, his hands laden with suitcases and duffel bags.

How long did she think she was staying?

"Vee's been helping fix up a house?" Adrien asked, his doubt evident.

"Yeah, she's done a lot of work. I don't know what I'd do without her." The way he was intently gazing at me let me know he meant the words beyond what I brought to the table in terms of home repair.

I broke his stare, unable to deal with the emotions he was expressing. "Need help?" I asked in a tone that made it clear I'd

ELIZABETH HAYLEY

rather swim with piranhas than assist her.

"Nah, I got it." She smiled as she hiked a bag up higher on her shoulder. "Maybe you could just show me which room is mine so I can put this stuff down."

"Oh yeah, of course," Owen said, leading the way into the house.

He'd fixed up a room for her, though I'd been happy to notice he hadn't put the same level of care into her room as he had mine.

Catty and petty? Sure. Did I care? Nope. There was no stained glass for wifey, and it thrilled me. Take that, Boyfriend Eloper!

Jesus, I'm truly losing it.

I needed to find a way past these . . . feelings. They were toxic and made me sad pretty much all the time. Taking a deep breath, I vowed to do better.

Until we walked in and Nattie said, "Are you sure it's safe to live here?" Then I was back to wanting to claw her eyes out.

Owen looked around confused, and I understood why. Compared to how the place had looked when I'd first moved in, it was a veritable palace.

Sure, there were exposed bulbs in the ceiling and some of the walls had spackle smeared across them, but there were no holes in the floors or vermin roaming the property. Owen had brought this old house a long way, and I opened my mouth to tell her as much, when Adrien spoke.

"Such a drama queen. This place is nice. Good bones and a lot of that old charm you don't see much of anymore."

I stared. Who was this person, and what had he done with my rough-around-the-edges cousin?

Nattie snorted. "What do you know about houses?"

"Clearly a lot more than you."

I wanted to add that it was probably because he spent a good deal of time casing them, but I'd just vowed to be a better person.

"Your room's this way," Owen said as he started up the stairs.

I wanted to make sure Natalia's comment hadn't hurt Owen's feelings but wasn't sure how to do that without making him vulnerable in front of my cousins. Not because they were horrible people, but because everything was a joke to them, and they'd exploit any opportunity to laugh at someone's expense.

Nattie and Adrien continued to bicker as we ascended the stairs, and I wondered if I could knock them down the steps in a way that appeared accidental.

Owen lumbered into Nattie's new room with her bags, and we followed. Everyone set what they were carrying down and looked around. I watched Nattie as she took in the room, ready to throat punch her if she was derogatory about Owen's efforts.

But instead, a small smile appeared on her lips. "This is nice."

"The crown molding in here is beautiful," Adrien said. The look on his face showed how impressed he was. Did he have a house kink I didn't know about?

"Yeah, a lot of the rooms have it. I just needed to patch it up in spots and repaint it," Owen explained.

"Definitely good bones," Adrien said, his voice almost a whisper, as if he'd been speaking to himself. "I'll go get the rest of the stuff."

"I'll help," Owen offered, following him out.

Which left Nattie and me alone.

We had so much to say to each other, but I wasn't in a place to say any of it right then. I acknowledged that I'd probably never be ready. But I'd force myself to talk to her. Eventually.

"Owen picked up some stuff for sandwiches," I said. "I'll start pulling it out, and then we can have lunch."

I turned to walk out of the room, but her voice stopped me.

"Are you gonna be mad at me forever?"

I stopped but didn't turn around. I didn't want lies between us, even when the truth hurt, so I responded accordingly. "I don't know. I hope not."

"I know it doesn't seem like it, but I really was just trying to help."

I sighed heavily and rubbed my eyes. "Do me a favor?"

"Anything," she replied immediately, like she was more than willing to do something, anything, for me.

"Don't try to help me anymore."

She was quiet for a long moment before she whispered, "Okay."

My heart hurt at the pain that laced that one word, but I was barely keeping it together myself. So instead, I muttered a "thanks" and left her room. But instead of going to the kitchen, I escaped to my room, barely getting the door closed before the first tear tracked down my cheek.

This was going to be tougher than I thought.

OWEN

Lunch was perhaps the tensest thing I'd ever been part of. Natalia kept trying to get a conversation going, Vee kept giving one-word answers, and Adrien kept looking like he was watching his favorite comedy unfold in front of him.

"So, Owen."

Oh God. In between bouts of being stonewalled by Vee, Natalia would turn and ask me questions she probably thought were casual getting-to-know-you topics, but it only seemed to aggravate Vee more. Which, really, Vee had only herself to blame because if *she'd* answer Natalia, I'd be off the hook.

"How old were you when you lost your virginity?"

Vee looked ready to levitate as her head spun three hundred and sixty degrees.

I, being the suave, confident guy I was, sputtered like a Renaissance man. "Wha...uh, I don't...why, why do you ask?"

Natalia's eyes sparkled as she put her elbows on the table and leaned closer. "Oh my God, you're not a virgin, are you?"

"That's—" I wiped my brow. When had I started sweating? "That's really none of your business."

Natalia smirked. "As your wife, I think I should know these things."

"Are you fucking kidding me?" Vee exploded.

"This is so great," Adrien quipped before he took another bite of his sandwich.

"Why the hell do you keep asking him this shit?" Vee asked, her tone hostile.

"Maybe if you'd do some of the talking, I wouldn't have to fill the silence," Natalia argued back.

"Or you could just keep your mouth shut for once."

Natalia smirked, but there was no mirth behind it. "How'd that work out for you?"

Vee stood and leaned menacingly toward Natalia. "What's that supposed to mean?"

"Maybe if you did more talking, and *listening*, this"— Natalia waved her hands around—"whole mess would never have happened."

"Oh, so this is my fault, huh? It's my fault that you constantly make the worst possible decision in any given situation? It's my fault that you got my boyfriend drunk and then suggested he marry you? It's my fault that your logic is so goddamn backward that you didn't see how marrying him would effectively be ruining what was between us instead of . . . whatever the hell you thought was going to happen?"

Natalia sat silently for a second as she stared at her plate. Then she stood and looked at Vee, not unkindly, but with an intensity I hadn't thought she was capable of. "No, none of those things are your fault. They're mine, and I own them. But you're not blameless here, Veronica. Instead of listening to Owen, really *hearing* him, you decided you knew better and made a decision that iced him out. I didn't ruin things between you. You'd already done that." With that, she turned and left the room without another word.

When I looked over at Vee, I saw that all the fight had gone out of her. "Excuse me," she murmured before fleeing the way her cousin had.

I slumped back in my seat, trying to wrap my head around what had just happened.

"Dude, can I move in too?" Adrien asked around a mouthful of chips. "Because the next three months are gonna be *epic*."

They'd certainly be that. I hoped we'd all survive.

Chapter Nine

OWEN

Despite Adrien saying he wanted to move in, I'd expected him to leave after lunch. I was mistaken. Instead, he puttered around the house and muttered to himself. He seemed to find the architecture of the place fascinating, and while I was glad to have someone appreciate my home, I kinda wished he'd leave so we could settle into ... whatever our new normal was going to look like.

Not that either of the girls had reappeared since the showdown in the kitchen. But they were family. That had to count for something. Right?

But having Adrien around was like pouring accelerant on a wildfire. He seemed to enjoy the hostility, and that wasn't the vibe we needed right now.

I was about to casually ask him when he was getting the hell out of my house when the doorbell rang. When I pulled the door open, Brody was on the other side smiling like a cartoon villain. Behind him were Aamee, Sophia, and Taylor.

"Where's your wife?" Brody asked as if he'd just asked to see someone's new puppy.

"Please don't call her that," I replied, my tone weary even to my own ears.

His brow scrunched up. "Why? Do Colombians find that term offensive or something?" He turned to look at Aamee as if she were a good litmus for what was socially acceptable.

She patted his back. "No, Owen's just being sensitive."

"*I'm* not being sensitive," I argued. "This whole situation is sensitive. For everyone."

Brody shrugged. "It's not sensitive for me." He then shouldered his way past me, the girls following.

I closed the door while I prayed to whatever higher power might be watching over this shitshow and begged them to intervene.

"Hey, man, I'm Brody," I heard from the other room.

"Hi. Adrien."

I followed their voices into the living room, where Brody and Adrien were making small talk. The girls were still by the entrance, and I stopped beside them.

"Who is this man who appears to be scoping out your house for valuables?" Aamee asked, thankfully in a low enough voice for Adrien not to have heard her.

Shit, was that why he'd been touching everything?

I dismissed the thought. Surely he wouldn't steal from his sister's husband.

"Natalia's brother."

"He's cute," Sophia remarked casually.

"If you like men who look like they chop up cars for parts," Aamee muttered.

"Stop being so judgy," Taylor admonished. "You don't know anything about him." She turned to me. "What's he like?"

I hesitated a moment before saying, "From what I've

heard, he's the type to chop up cars for parts."

Aamee looked smug as Taylor rolled her eyes and murmured, "Whatever."

"Hey, babe," Brody yelled. When he had Aamee's—and all of our—attention, he jerked a thumb at Adrien. "He says he can get us a deal on booze for the wedding. We'd just have to pay him up front in cash."

Aamee arched one perfectly manicured eyebrow at Taylor, who huffed in response. Then she strode over toward the two men. "The venue provides the alcohol as part of the wedding package. But thanks for the very sweet offer." She said "very sweet" in a way that made it clear she knew exactly what Adrien was proposing and she wasn't for it.

Adrien shrugged in response before turning toward Sophia and Taylor. A wide grin split his face, which, I had to admit, made his already handsome features even more appealing. His white teeth set against his tan skin gave him a charisma I was sure I'd never possess.

Then he opened his mouth, and whatever charm he'd possessed evaporated. "Either of you single?"

Sophia gave him a quelling look. "No."

He shoved his hands in his pockets and grinned even wider. "That's a shame. I was hoping I'd find someone to... show me around."

"Around where?" I asked. "You've already seen the house."

He smirked at me in a way that made me feel like I'd missed something. Before Adrien could say anything else, Natalia appeared in the doorway. She was dressed in jean shorts and a blue top that I'd have classified as more of a bra since it didn't cover her shoulders or her stomach, but more just wrapped around her chest. Her makeup was also done.

"Oh, are you heading out with Adrien?" I asked.

"No, silly," she said, smiling at me, making her look remarkably like her brother. "I came down to meet your friends." She quickly stepped forward and extended her hand to the girls and Brody, introducing herself. Then she asked, "Does anyone want anything to drink?"

I stood there perplexed. It was like she'd suddenly transformed into the PG-13 version of Mrs. Cleaver.

They all shared a brief look before Sophia said, "No, we're fine, thanks."

"Are you hungry? I can see what snacks we have," Natalia offered.

I looked over at Adrien to try to get a read on whether he knew what was happening. It wasn't that Natalia had ever been outwardly rude, per se. But she'd never seemed like the type to take hosting so seriously.

Adrien was looking at her like she'd just offered everyone a severed head to munch on, so I figured I was safe in my assessment that this wasn't typical behavior.

It looked like Sophia was about to decline again when Brody piped up. "I could eat."

"There's a surprise," Aamee said. "I'll feed you later."

"No, it's okay. I'll bring out some things." Natalia disappeared in the direction of the kitchen, leaving all of us staring at each other.

"She seems nice," Sophia said, her words careful and measured.

"She's getting us food. What's not to love?" Brody said before turning back to Adrien. "Do you know anything about tuxes?"

I tuned out the rest of that conversation and instead told

the girls I'd be back, and then I followed Natalia to the kitchen.

She was moving around like a squirrel on meth, opening cabinets and drawers like one of them contained a life-saving antidote she desperately needed.

"You okay?" I asked carefully.

She whirled around and smiled when she saw me, though it looked strained. "Me? Oh yeah, I'm fine. Never better. Just"—she looked around the kitchen at all the open cabinets— "looking for snacks."

"You know you don't have to feed them, right? They're actually kind of like seagulls. Once you give them food, they'll never leave, so it may be better if you don't."

She turned so her back was to me. "Just trying to be a good host."

That was when it hit me. She was nervous. For whatever reason, she clearly wanted to make a good impression. Maybe it was because she figured my friends would automatically hate her because of what happened, or maybe it was because making my friends like her would further piss Vee off. Whatever the reason, Natalia was struggling, and it didn't seem fair to leave her that way.

I went over to the fridge and pulled out a jar of salsa I'd opened a few days before. Then I went to the pantry and pulled out a bag of tortilla chips before dumping all of it into bowls. I handed it to Natalia with a smile.

"This'll tide them over."

She took the bowls and gave me a small smile. "Thanks."

"Sure thing."

When Natalia left to deliver the food, I pulled my phone out of my back pocket and sent a text to Vee.

Some of the gang is here. You wanna
come down?

The three dots appeared and disappeared a couple of times before words finally came through.

Is Natalia there?

I blew out a breath, wondering if Vee was going to spend the next three months hiding in her room.

Yeah.

Her reply was instantaneous.

Be down in five.

I stared at my phone, confused. Before sliding it back into my pocket, I came to one undebatable truth.

I really didn't understand women.

Chapter Ten

VERONICA

When Owen texted me that Natalia was hanging out with our friends, I knew I had to get down there. While seeing her wasn't high on my list of things I wanted to do, letting her replace me in my friend group was even lower.

As I looked at myself in the mirror and freshened up my makeup so it didn't look like I'd spent the past hour crying, I wondered if this paranoid, overly emotional person was who I'd be from here on out. As I took stock of my reflection, I realized I didn't like this Vee very much.

I also had to concede that, even though it had pissed me off to hear it, Natalia had been right earlier—I was the root cause of all of this mess.

But she was my cousin, damn it. Did she have to make the whole thing totally FUBAR?

Taking a deep breath, I vowed to do better. With everything. Or at least I'd try.

I arrived in the living room to see Natalia talking animatedly to Taylor and Sophia, both of whom were wide-eyed and looking a bit shell-shocked. I couldn't help the tiny quirk of my lips. Natalia was a force to interact with.

Aamee was hovering worriedly next to Brody as he spoke to Adrien. That was probably wise considering Adrien was probably capable of convincing the Pope to commit petty crime, all while making it sound completely legit.

Owen was standing between the two groups, looking back and forth between them a bit frantically, as if he was expecting all hell to break loose any second.

Smart man.

But then his gaze caught on mine and he seemed to instantly calm—his shoulders relaxed, and the creases on his brow disappeared. He looked at me with that soft look I'd come to love because it was reserved just for me.

"Hi, guys," I said as I walked farther into the room.

Sophia and Taylor looked relieved to see me, and I tried not to be overjoyed by that.

"Hey," Sophia said. "We were just talking to your cousin about her hair care routine."

My eyes darted over to Natalia of their own volition, and what I saw there was somewhat surprising. She looked... nervous. Whether she was nervous I was going to start in on her in front of company or because of the company itself, I wasn't sure.

I turned my attention to the girls and smiled. "She's definitely the one to go to if you have any questions. She's been perfecting that routine since she was ten and thought putting rubber cement in her hair would make it shiny."

I'd meant the anecdote to be a fond reminiscence, but once I'd let it slip, I immediately regretted it. What if Nattie thought I was telling the story to embarrass her? That I was being petty instead of trying to build a bridge, no matter how wobbly that sucker might be.

But thankfully, she laughed. "It seemed like a good idea at the time." She sobered as she seemed to realize what she said.

That was Nattie in a nutshell—things always *seemed* to be a good idea. Unfortunately, they rarely were.

"What have you guys been up to?" I asked them in an attempt to redirect the conversation.

"Not much," Taylor replied. "Brody wanted to come over and meet Natalia and Adrien, so we tagged along."

I would've thought it odd how they traveled in groups if that wasn't how they'd all always been.

We all fell into conversation after that. I tried to distract Brody every time Adrien talked about "knowing a guy" for everything from wedding flowers to honeymoon time-shares, and I tried to interject whenever Taylor and Sophia started to glaze over as Nattie prattled on about her skin care routine and her obsession with Jake Paul. But when Aamee and Adrien found common ground in the fine art of tax evasion, I elected to sit back and watch like everyone else.

"There's nothing wrong with not declaring all your income," Adrien said.

Aamee nodded, but Taylor broke in. "Except it's illegal and, therefore, definitionally wrong."

Aamee waved Taylor off and turned back to Adrien. "Lawyer," she said sarcastically.

Adrien widened his eyes as if that explained a lot. "Corporations hide money all the time. But if I hide a couple grand, I'm looking at a federal charge. Ridiculous."

"It's so true. My mom used to launder money through shell companies like it was nothing."

"Such a double standard. She sounds like a boss, though."

"She is. Both how you mean it and literally." Aamee seemed to be contemplating something before she continued. "You know, if you ever want some help moving cash around, I know a guy—"

"*And* on that note, I think it's time we left," Brody interjected as he stood.

Aamee joined him in standing, but she made no other moves to leave as she stared at Brody in disbelief. "You were literally just talking about getting our centerpieces from a guy named Cliff in the Bronx, but *my* conversation makes you want to leave?"

"I wasn't talking about other girls," Brody argued.

"What?" Aamee asked, clearly confused.

I'm with ya, sister.

I was used to Brody making no sense, but this was extreme even for him.

"You were talking about some guy."

"I was?"

Brody looked at Aamee like she wasn't too bright, which, if I'd been Aamee, I would've been highly insulted by.

"Yeah, you said you knew a guy."

Aamee threw her hands up. "I know lots of guys. Drew, Ransom, Carter. Why are you making a big deal out of this one?"

"Those aren't guys—they're our friends."

"Well, I'll be sure to let them know that their friendship with you strips them of their manhood," she said snarkily. "And I can know whoever I want to, Brody Mason. Just because we're getting married doesn't mean you can control me."

Natalia leaned toward me. "Did we look this stupid when

we were arguing earlier?" she whispered.

"Probably. But that was a lot less fun than this."

She was quiet for a few seconds before she said, "It wasn't fun for me either."

I turned so I could look at her. "Then maybe we should not do it again."

"I'd really like that." She was smiling widely, and I wanted to hate the tiny tendril of happiness that unfurled inside me at having made things right with her, but I couldn't.

I went back to watching Aamee and Brody bicker, thinking how Brody's stupidity had inadvertently helped me once again.

Chapter Eleven

OWEN

"Do you know where I can find a job?" Natalia asked me.

I'd been sitting in the kitchen making a list of things I needed to bring home from the hardware store when she'd startled me with her question.

"Uh, not off the top of my head, no," I replied.

She sighed in that heavily dramatic way she often displayed.

"It's summer," I added. "I'm sure a lot of places are hiring seasonal help."

"But how do you, like, get one?"

"Get one what?" I could've sworn sometimes that this girl spoke a different language. One that blended Valley Girl vernacular with mob family delivery.

"A job." A *duh* at the end was clearly implied.

I scratched the back of my neck. "Well, you can get one a couple of different ways. You can scroll through online classifieds, you can go to Lazarus and look at the employment boards they have scattered around the quad, or you can walk into places and ask them."

She was quiet as she pondered that for a second, so I asked, "Have you never had a job before?"

"I have, but never one I got for myself. It's always been my mom or dad telling me they're tired of seeing me around the house and sending me to some store or something that a friend of theirs owns. This time, they told me I had to get one, but they're not going to help me find it." She crossed her arms over her chest. "They're so hard on me sometimes."

I let her last comment go and focused on reality. "Okay, well, of the jobs you've had, which did you like the best?"

She tapped a manicured finger against her chin as she thought. Finally she said, "I never really liked any of them."

For fuck's sake. "Was there one you hated the least?"

"I once babysat a guy's pet turtle for a week. That wasn't too bad. I got to stay at his house. But then I found his BDSM room, and he called my parents, angry that I'd violated his privacy. How was I supposed to know he'd see my TikTok about his dungeon? I didn't even know he followed me."

"Wow, that's . . . a lot to unpack." I took a second to figure out where I took the conversation from there. "I don't think you're going to find a lot of turtle-sitting gigs. Is there anything else you think you'd like? What about somewhere that sells clothes or makeup or something?"

"I'm not a very good liar."

"Why would you have to be a good liar to sell makeup?"

"Because people usually ask how they look, and they usually don't want to hear the truth."

"But that would be your job. To make them look better."

Natalia shook her head. "I'm not qualified to be a miracle worker."

That was clearly a dead end, so I changed directions. "We

have some friends who may have some contacts. Drew runs an outdoor bar. Do you think you'd be good at serving drinks?"

"No, I'm only good at drinking them."

"Vee is working at a summer camp."

She looked at me like I was stupid for even suggesting it. "Next."

"Um, well…tell you what. Why don't you meet me at the hardware store after my shift, and we'll walk around the neighborhood and see if anything jumps out at you?"

"Like a mugger?" she asked, horrified.

"No, I meant we can see if anything catches your attention. If so, we can go in and ask if they're hiring and fill out an application."

She clapped her hands together. "That sounds so fun! Like a treasure hunt, except the treasure is something that makes you miserable, but you need to find it anyway."

"That was actually a pretty astute summary of the American working experience."

She smiled in a way that made me think she knew I'd complimented her but wasn't sure exactly what I'd said. "Okay, great. What time is your shift over?"

"Four. Hopefully that'll give us time to stop in a few places before any of the shops close. It's a pretty busy neighborhood, so I'm sure we'll find something. I'll text you the address."

"Great. See you at five."

"Four!" I called after her as she bounded out of the kitchen. I included the time in the text, just in case.

Vee had already left for work at Safe Haven, so I sent her a text too, asking if she wanted to meet us. She had the early shift this week, so she should be done by three or so. Maybe helping Natalia get a job would help dissipate any of the remaining awkwardness between them.

They hadn't sniped at each other since that first day, and they weren't actively avoiding each other, but it was obvious things were still tense. They didn't speak beyond exchanging casual pleasantries, and they never elected to spend time together unless I orchestrated it.

My phone buzzed, and I looked down at it.

Natalia ... my cousin Natalia ... wants to get a job?

> *I think her parents are making her.*

Ah, that makes more sense.

> *So you in?*

Sure. I'll come to the hardware store after my shift. Should be there by three thirty or so.

I sent her a thumbs-up emoji and pocketed my phone, thinking positive thoughts in hopes that, for once, it would work.

VERONICA

Taking a deep breath, I pulled open the door of the hardware store and pushed myself through the threshold. I hadn't gotten here as early as I'd planned. One of the counselors had been late, and then I'd ambled over to the store more slowly than was necessary, anxious about what the rest of the day might bring. This would be the first time just the three of us would hang out socially since the party. And we hadn't even done much of that then.

I'd given myself a pep talk on my way to the store. I would be normal. I wouldn't be catty or petty. I'd make the same effort Owen was making to get us all to a place where the threat of physical violence wasn't constantly looming. Even though I was sure that last one only applied to me.

I heard Nattie's laughter as soon as I entered, and I followed it to the counter, where I saw her almost bent in half as she rested her arms on the top. Owen stood on the other side smiling as he tidied up.

Her pose looked flirtatious, and I got immediately defensive about it, but I forced myself to calm. I knew these people. Owen wasn't interested in Nattie. Nattie wasn't interested in Owen. And even if she was, she wouldn't go there. Marry him? Evidently yes. Steal him away from me? No. Even though we hadn't been very close in years, I still knew her well enough to know she wouldn't do that. But knowing something and trusting it were two very different things.

Still, I forced a smile to my face and approached them. "Hey. Were you guys waiting long?"

Nattie turned toward me and smiled cautiously. "Nah, I just got here a few minutes ago."

"And I still have fifteen minutes left in my shift," Owen added.

"Don't keep the ladies waiting," Mark yelled from… somewhere. I'd only met the man a couple of times, but his voice was distinctive, raspy and gruff as if he'd swallowed a cactus.

"You sure?" Owen asked, already removing his apron.

"Yeah, sure." He muttered something else, but it was too low for any of us to hear.

"Okay, see you tomorrow."

There was no response to Owen that time, and he didn't seem to expect one because he wasted no time in leading us out of the store.

"So where do we start?" Nattie asked once we made it outside.

"Have you thought any more about what kind of job you'd like to have?" Owen asked her.

"Was I supposed to?" she replied, looking confused.

"Uh, well, no, I guess not," Owen hedged, making me smile. It showed how little he knew Nattie that he thought she'd take initiative on the day.

It wasn't that she was purposefully being difficult. It likely hadn't occurred to her that planning ahead might help this process along.

"Why don't we just walk and look for help wanted signs or places that look interesting to you?" I suggested.

They agreed, so we made our way up the street, discussing each store as we passed. It was a good area to look in—there were tons of shops, restaurants, and businesses for her to choose from. We also stopped to take a few pictures, since the judge was requiring them to document their relationship.

"What about that diner?" Owen suggested.

I gave the place a once-over before looking at Nattie. "Have you ever worked in food service?" I couldn't help but think back to the time I'd tried to work at the Yard. I wasn't sure Nattie would be any more suited for it than I was, but what did I know?

"You mean a waitress?" she asked.

We nodded.

"No. Mom won't even let me carry food to the dinner table."

Owen looked at me and smirked. "Must be a family trait."

I pointed at him. "That's enough out of you."

He laughed, and I couldn't help but smile as well.

"I feel like I'm missing something," Nattie said with a small smile of her own.

"It's nothing," I said, waving it off, but Owen launched into the story, the jerk.

"Vee tried working at a place our friend manages, and she was ... Well, let's just say they asked her not to come back."

I squawked. "That's not what happened!" I sniffed. "I just made the decision that it would be best for all involved if I didn't work there anymore."

"She was a one-woman mercenary. Her target? Anything breakable."

I slapped him playfully. "I did my best."

"Yes, you did. That's what made it all so sad."

I couldn't help the laughter that burst out of me then. "Okay, okay, I sucked as a server. But Nattie may not. You want to give it a try?"

She eyed the building warily. "I guess." Her voice didn't inspire confidence, but we made our way over.

The diner was small and cramped. It was also packed. Servers moved about quickly and efficiently as they refilled cups, dropped off food, and cleaned up tables. It was like restaurant triage.

"Can I help you?" a young girl at the register asked.

Nattie straightened her shoulders. "Yes," she said. She went to take a step closer to the counter, but her shoe caught on a mat on the floor, causing it to pull up from the ground. A server carrying a large tray of food tripped on it, causing the tray to go careening forward.

We watched in slow motion as the plates filled with someone's dinner crashed to the floor, directly next to a table. Some of the food ended up on the customer's shoes.

The place went still and quiet as everyone stared at the scene beside us.

Nattie turned back to the girl. "On second thought, I think I'm good." She then spun around and hightailed it out of there, Owen and I close on her heels.

"I don't think that would've been a good fit," she said after we'd gotten a few yards away from the diner.

"That's okay. We'll find something that is," Owen said, ever the optimist.

Over the course of the next hour or so, Nattie had applied at a florist where I was pretty sure the woman had immediately tossed Nattie's application after Nattie had told her fake flowers were better than real ones, a boutique where Nattie had immediately asked if employees got a discount before looking around the place and muttering, "Never mind," a pet store where Nattie had been making a good impression until she asked if she'd actually have to touch the animals, and a bookstore where she announced she hadn't read anything since her mom had made her read a book for summer school once.

Things were not looking good, and I could tell even Owen was ready to wave the white flag.

I was about to suggest we get dinner and pick this up a different day, when Nattie spoke.

"What about that place?"

I followed her line of sight to see an auto repair shop. "There?" I asked, not able to keep the incredulity from my voice.

She shrugged. "They have a help wanted sign up."

"Have you ever worked in a garage before?" Owen asked.

"No, but I haven't worked at any of the other places I've applied either."

"Yeah, but working on cars is a trade," he explained. "You'd need a lot of training to do that kind of work."

"We don't know they're looking for a mechanic," she reasoned. "Maybe they just need someone to do . . . something else," she said, clearly at a loss for what else might be needed in a garage. "We won't know if we don't ask, right?" She took off in the direction of the garage.

Owen and I stared at each other before following after her. A bell above the door tinkled as we entered. Nattie went directly to the counter while Owen and I held back.

There was a man in a blue work shirt behind the counter talking to a customer in a white polo shirt and khaki pants.

"Be right with you," Blue Shirt said to Nattie before turning his attention back to his customer. "I don't know what else to tell you, man. They don't make those wheels anymore."

"That's ridiculous. The car's barely four years old."

"But they discontinued them because they have a tendency to crack. Which you found out the hard way."

"I can't have one wheel different from the other three."

Blue Shirt sighed. "Like I explained, new wheels are covered on all four tires since the ones you currently have were recalled."

"But the replacements you showed me are ugly. The ones I have are way nicer."

"The factory will reimburse you the cost of the current wheels if you want to pay the difference to upgrade—"

"I shouldn't have to pay anything for new rims."

The two men continued to argue back and forth, and it didn't look like they were going to stop anytime soon. It was probably best for Nattie to come back. Or forget about working here in the first place. I was about to step forward and tug her back to me when she reached across the counter and pulled a sheet of paper in front of her.

"Wow, are these the new wheels?" Nattie said.

Both men fell immediately silent as they turned to look at her.

She looked up at the irate man in the white shirt and smiled. "These are sexy. Why don't you want 'em?"

"It's not that I don't want them," he said, running a hand over the back of his head as if he were nervous to be on the receiving end of her attention.

"Then what is it?" she asked.

"I just don't think I should have to pay more for them. It's not my fault the rim cracked."

Nattie turned to the man in the blue shirt. "Is it your fault?"

The man's eyes twinkled in what seemed to be amusement. "Nope."

"Oh." Nattie looked back at the wheels for a second as both men looked at her. Then, she pushed the paper back in front of the man. "I get not having the money. I guess I assumed since you were dressed so professionally that you could afford them. Sorry for butting in."

"Oh, no, it's not that I can't afford them," the man quickly spluttered. "It's more . . . the principle of the thing."

Nattie's eyes narrowed like she was confused. "What principle is that?"

"Excuse me?" the man said, sounding as confused as I was.

"Well, usually when people say that, they're standing up for something. A moral high ground or whatever. I was just wondering what exactly it was you were standing for?"

The man's mouth opened and closed a few times as he clearly struggled to find a suitable reply.

When he didn't say anything, Nattie continued. "I think it's amazing you can get these rims without having to pay full price for them. I bet not a lot of people can even afford them. You may have one of the only cars around that has them."

She made it sound like this was an achievement akin to winning a Nobel Prize.

The man smiled. "Ya think?"

She gestured to Blue Shirt, who said, "They're specialty rims, so you won't see many of them on the road."

The customer thought for a moment longer before he said, "Okay. I'll take these rims."

"Great. I'll go get you the paperwork for claiming the reimbursement for the broken wheels." He started to walk away before turning back to Nattie. "Can you wait another couple minutes?"

"Sure," she said with a flirty smile that made the guy shake his head in amusement as he walked away.

It took a bit longer for him to finish with the customer and set up a time for him to come back and collect his car, but when the uptight guy was gone, the man in the blue shirt spread his hands on the counter and grinned at Nattie.

"Well, that was impressive."

She shrugged. "Getting guys to spend money they don't really wanna part with is kind of my thing."

"That's a handy talent."

She hummed in agreement. "Maybe one that could be used around here?"

His eyebrows shot up. "You looking for a job?"

"Yup."

"Any references?"

She winced. "Not any good ones."

"Uh," I interrupted. "We could give her personal references."

Nattie lit up at my offer. I guess she was pleasantly surprised that I'd vouch for her. I might have even been a bit surprised myself. But she was my cousin, and if I could help her, I would.

"Friends of yours?" he asked, motioning to us with a nod of his head.

"Family," she replied.

He considered her a moment before saying, "I'll have to run a background check."

Nattie nodded in understanding.

"And if that comes back okay, I'd be willing to hire you on a trial basis. We'll see if you can do the parts of the job that *don't* entail swindling men out of their money."

Nattie put her hands on her hips. "I wasn't aware I was swindling him. Do you sell shitty products here?"

The man laughed. "I think you're gonna fit in just fine here. I'm Nate, by the way."

"Natalia." They shook, and then Nate invited Natalia back to his office to fill out some paperwork. Before she went, she looked back at us.

"There's a café on the corner," Owen said. "We'll wait for you there, and then we can go to dinner to celebrate."

"Or," Nate said from behind us, "the guys are always up for hitting happy hour. You can get to know them a bit. We only have an hour left before closing, and the paperwork takes a little while."

Natalia's eyes sparked.

"Nattie," I warned. I didn't think it was a great idea for her to go out with a bunch of strange men, even if she would be working with them.

"You're all welcome to come," Nate added.

Natalia turned back to me and appraised me for a moment. Her attention made me fidgety. "I think you two should go to dinner and celebrate without me."

Owen looked at me, confusion clear in the furrowing of his brow. "We don't have anything to celebrate without you."

"That doesn't have to be the case," she replied.

I sighed. "Is this just your way of convincing us to let you go to a bar with a bunch of guys you don't know?"

"Hey," Nate interjected. "We have two other women on staff. We're an open-minded bunch."

I held up a hand. "Sorry for stereotyping."

He nodded once, which I took to mean he accepted my apology.

"Vee," Nattie said as she put her hands on my shoulders. "Go on a date with Owen."

"A date, huh?" I said, letting my eyes drift over to Owen, who was shifting from one foot to the other as he watched us.

"Yes. A real date. With kissing." She pretended to whisper the last part, but it was so loud, everyone in the room heard.

I mirrored her pose, putting my hands on her shoulders.

"Text me when you're on your way home?"

She rolled her eyes, but she couldn't hide her smile. She was pleased I cared enough to worry about her. "Okay, Mom."

"You're such a brat."

She laughed, leaned forward and pressed a quick kiss to my cheek, and then followed Nate, giving us a wave over her shoulder as she disappeared into the back.

"We could go with them to happy hour," Owen said, pulling my focus back to him. "If you'd feel better going with her."

I cast a quick look at the door before facing him again. "Nah. She's a big girl. If she can handle Bronx men, she can handle these guys."

"Okay. So, uh, did you wanna... I mean, I know she said we should go to dinner, but if you'd rather... we can... I mean, I'd love to go, but if you—"

"Owen," I interrupted softly.

"Yeah?"

"I'd love to go to dinner with you too."

His answering smile was bright and wide. I wanted to do whatever I could to keep it on his face. And I figured dinner was a good place to start.

Chapter Twelve

VERONICA

We decided on a small bistro down the street from the garage instead of the café. They had outdoor seating lit primarily by twinkling lights strewn overhead and lampposts hanging over the road. It was cozy, and I was thankful for a bit of darkness to cover my nerves.

Even when Owen and I had been falling for each other, we hadn't really gone on any dates. We lived together, so it had never occurred to either of us. But now I was beginning to see it for the oversight it was.

There was something different about being out with him like this. My belly filled with butterflies as we sat across from each other and discussed our days. There was a kind of tension filling the space between us, but it was the good kind—the kind that let me know that we each cared about the other and wanted tonight to go well.

Our meal was filling and delicious, and the company was even better. The further we got into the evening, the more we each loosened up, until it was the old Owen and the old Vee giving each other shit and sharing funny stories.

Owen insisted on paying the tab, assuring me that it wasn't male posturing but rather that he'd been the one to mention dinner, so he wanted to pay this time as long as it wasn't insulting to my autonomy. He was the cutest feminist ever.

Neither of us were ready for the night to end, so we decided to wander around a bit more and watch the evening bring an entirely different city to life. When I moved closer to Owen to avoid a rowdy group of guys probably heading to the bar for the night, the back of my hand brushed Owen's.

And when he clasped it in his and threaded our fingers together, it was like something else within me settled, as if pieces of a larger puzzle were slowly slotting back into place. We were slowly becoming whole again.

And maybe it was silly of me to hope that one night could fix everything. Realistically, I knew that was unlikely. But it could put us back on track.

"Did you go out a lot when you were in undergrad?" he asked as college students walked past us, laughing in large groups as they headed out for the evening.

"Eh, more so my first two years. I buckled down junior year. I went out here and there, but definitely more in a social way than in a let-me-get-drunk-off-my-ass way. What about you?"

He shrugged. "I guess. I tried to do what it seemed everyone else was doing. Joined a frat, partied most weekends, but none of it felt . . . like me. Which would probably surprise everyone back home, because I was definitely wilder in high school. Maybe I got it out of my system early."

"You also took a gap year, which maybe made you a little more mature."

He laughed. "I don't think anyone would say what I did during that year was mature."

I laughed too. "I can only imagine." Part of me wanted to ask for the particulars, but another part knew that wasn't the Owen I wanted to get to know. There would hopefully be plenty of time to share our pasts once we got the present sorted out.

"I gotta tell my parents about Natalia," he said, his voice laced with trepidation. The thought seemingly came out of nowhere, but I was sure it had been on his mind since the judge made it one of the stipulations of the annulment.

"What do you think they'll say?" I asked, giving his hand a squeeze.

He sighed. "I honestly don't know. On one hand, this is very on-brand for the old Owen, so they may not even be all that surprised. But... I dunno. My parents and grandparents are all pretty big on the sanctity of marriage. They all joke around with their spouses, but at the end of the day, they take their vows seriously." He was quiet for a second before he whispered, "I think they're going to be really disappointed."

"We'll get through it," I said, lightly bumping my shoulder against his.

He whipped his face in my direction. "*We* will?" His eyes burned with intensity, as if my next words would make or break him. It was a heady power to wield.

"Yeah. We."

He tried to hide his smile, but I saw it before he faced forward again, making my own lips tip up at the corners.

"Will *we* also come to marriage counseling?" he said, his voice clearly teasing.

"Ugh, I forgot about that. You're on your own there."

"Traitor."

"You're the one who went off and married my cousin. You have only yourself to blame."

He looked at me again, seeming like he wanted to say something but was holding back.

"What?" I asked.

"I'm glad you can joke about it now."

Breaking his gaze, I focused on the street in front of us as I processed his words. On some level, the ordeal *wasn't* funny—would probably never be funny. But at the same time, sometimes we had to take the gravity of a situation away to make it bearable.

"I'm sure I'll have my days where I'll still be pissed about it. But . . . I'm getting there."

"Thank you," he said.

His words took me by surprise. "For what?"

"For being honest about how you feel. If you pretended things were better when they weren't, we'd be trying to build a relationship on a pile of resentments, and it would never work. And I desperately want us to work. Not that I'll push," he hurried to add. "If you're not feeling it, I understand. I'd never try to steamroll your feelings, or—"

"Owen," I interrupted, pulling him to a stop so we could face each other fully.

He gazed at me like he was prepared to hang on every word. Had anyone ever valued me this much? Would there ever be another man like him? I wasn't sure I wanted to find out.

"You know that your wants and feelings are just as valid, right?"

He nodded, but it had a halting quality to it that said he wasn't truly sure what I was getting at.

"Sometimes I worry you make it so much about me that you're not thinking about what you need in return."

"But"—he looked adorably confused—"I just need you."

I stepped closer, my chest brushing up against him. "That's very sweet. But relationships are about compromise. Don't let me steamroll you into doing all the fixing. We both have work to do."

He nodded. "Maybe we should go to counseling after all." His tone was teasing, but his voice was low, almost a whisper against my lips.

"Let's tackle one relationship in therapy at a time," I replied.

"Okay."

We continued to stand in each other's space in the middle of the sidewalk. People were probably giving us dirty looks, but I didn't have it in me to care.

"Owen," I murmured.

"Yeah?"

I smiled. "Kiss me already."

His smile met mine in a careful press of lips that felt as fragile as our relationship.

But it only took a second for the kiss to deepen, for it to become something both new and familiar. We stood there, lost in each other, having what I considered to be our second first kiss.

OWEN

The date with Vee had been . . . everything. I'd been so careful not to push, not to have any expectations, that for all the things

I wanted to happen in the same night was almost beyond belief.

We'd eventually found our way home after walking for a while longer. It wasn't late by normal standards, but we'd both had long days. And I didn't want to mess up what had started between us by going too far. So I walked her to her bedroom door, gave her a chaste kiss on the cheek, and wished her a good night.

She'd smiled softly and wished me the same before disappearing into her room.

I'd spent a while staring at my ceiling, replaying the night in my mind before finally drifting off to a restful sleep.

When I awoke the next morning, I knew it was time to start putting things in motion.

I was sure it seemed like I'd been doing all I could to make the annulment happen, but the reality was, I'd been dragging my feet. Not because I didn't want it to happen, but because it was easier to go through the motions than to take active steps to fixing things.

But the possibility of Vee and me getting back on track lit a fire underneath me. And the first step was telling my parents.

My parents had always been early risers, so I didn't hesitate to call after I made a quick trip to the bathroom. It rang twice before the call connected.

"Who's this?" my mom asked, her voice intentionally curious.

"I get it. I haven't called recently. I'm sorry."

"That's a very long name. Do you have a nickname?"

"Mom," I groaned.

"Hmm, I had a son who used to call me Mom, but he's been lost to me now for going on . . . a year? Two? It's so hard to keep track."

"Two weeks. It's been two weeks since we last spoke."

"That doesn't sound right. I'm sure it's been longer."

I rolled my eyes. My mom came across as stoic, but she was a dramatic crybaby underneath. "You told me all about having to take Grandma for her mammogram. Which I know just happened because she texted me about having a titty ache. Which, honestly, I really don't appreciate having to hear about. None of my friends have to hear about that kind of stuff from their grandparents. I think it's time to take her phone away. She's clearly losing it."

"Yes, it is odd she'd text a virtual stranger about her breast health."

"Mom," I warned.

"Okay, okay, fine. Jeez, you're no fun anymore."

If she thought I was no fun because of that, wait until I told her I was married.

"Is Dad there?"

"Yeah, he should be coming down for breakfast any minute. Why?" Her voice was suspicious. It wasn't that I didn't get along with my dad or avoided talking to him. But it was normally easier to tell her what I had to say and let her relay it to him. Asking for him was definitely out of the ordinary.

"I just had something to tell you both. Can you call him and then put me on speaker?"

"You called the house phone. I don't even think it has a speaker."

"It does. There's a button on the base that says speaker."

I heard some shuffling before her voice came through the line again. "I don't see it."

Praying to the heavens for strength, I walked her through how to put the speaker on.

"Well, would ya look at that?" my mom said. "Learn something new every day."

"I'll pretend to be impressed by your *landline* knowledge."

"I can tell you're being snide, and I don't appreciate it. You're the one who called that number. You could've called my cell phone."

"You never answer it," I argued.

"Doesn't mean you can't call it."

Christ, she was impossible sometimes. "Is Dad down yet?"

"What? No...oh wait...here he is. Your son's on the phone," she said, the last part obviously to my dad.

"I have a son?"

"Not you too," I groaned.

"You do," my mom said. "His name is Owen. Do you remember?"

My dad hummed. "I have a vague memory of teaching a little blond-haired boy to ride a bike, throw a football, drive a car, and I definitely remember teaching him to call his damn parents once in a while. But it's all fuzzy now. It's been so, so long."

"I'm sorry, okay? If I promise to call more, can we stop whatever this is?"

"Who's that?"

I silently cursed when I heard Grandma Jimi's voice.

"Owen," my mom answered.

"Never heard of him," Grandma replied.

"You realize all this makes me want to call even less, right?"

"We're just teasing. Don't get your boxers in a twist," Grandma snarked.

"So to what do we owe the pleasure of this call?" my mom asked.

"I, well, I...uh...I have some news." Planning to tell them and actually going through with it were two very different things. I'd also hoped to only speak to my mom and dad. My grandma never met a situation she didn't actively try to make worse, and that wasn't really what I was going for right now.

"Spit it out, for God's sake," Grandma said. "Your mom's burning the bacon waitin' on ya."

"You see, I kinda...did a thing."

"What thing?" Mom asked.

"An illegal thing?" my dad added. "You don't need bail money, do ya?"

"What? Jesus, no."

"Don't take the Lord's name in vain," Mom reprimanded.

"The *Lord's*...are you serious right now? You got me suspended from Sunday school for letting me wear a *Jesus is my Homeboy* shirt, and you wanna lecture me about the sanctity of His name?"

"There was nothing wrong with that shirt. That teacher was a shrew."

"The shirt was a little disrespectful," my dad said.

"You better remember who cooks your meals before you go picking sides. I've heard arsenic is real easy to conceal," Mom warned.

Bickering ensued, and as I listened, the anxiety and irritation bubbled until I exploded. "I got married!"

Silence. I wasn't sure I'd ever heard my family go quiet this instantly.

Finally, my mom spoke. "You and Veronica got married and didn't invite us?"

Oh shit.

"Was her family there?" Grandma asked, a thread of hurt in her voice.

"Were you drunk?" my dad asked. At least one person was on the right track.

"I, uh, well, it's complicated."

"Tying yourself to another person for the rest of your life normally is," Mom said.

The glib scoff was out of my mouth before I registered what I was doing. "We're not staying married. We're trying to get an annulment."

Silence again. Then . . . chaos. All their voices erupted at once.

"An annulment?" Mom asked.

"I thought you really liked that girl?" added Grandma.

"Who's going to pay for that?" asked Dad, ever the pragmatist.

I rubbed my head. "Can you guys just let me explain?"

The rabble subsided, and my mom sniffed. "Well, go on then."

"I didn't marry Vee."

Some indignant squawks erupted, but they thankfully quieted again.

"I married her cousin."

"Jesus Christ," my mother muttered. I wanted to call her out on her words, but for my safety, I decided against it. She wasn't above driving up from Virginia to murder me.

"What the hell is going on up there?" Grandma asked. "Y'all got some kind of . . . *Deliverance* shit going on."

"I married Vee's cousin, not my own," I replied.

"Polygamy, then. You know your grandpa and I—"

"Please," my mom interrupted. "Spare us all the rest of that sentence." She took a deep breath before continuing. "We raised you better than this. We raised him better than this, didn't we?" I assumed the last question was directed at my dad.

"We sure as hell did. Owen, explain. Now."

So I did. I relayed the whole embarrassing tale, and when I finished, I was met with silence.

"You guys still there?"

"I don't even know what to say," Mom replied.

That wasn't good. The woman *always* had something to say.

"Veronica actually came back to live with you? After you betrayed her like this?" Grandma asked.

I winced. Having my actions thrown at me still hurt like a physical blow. "She did. We're . . . working through it."

"I'd be working through your internal organs if you'd done that to me," Grandma sniped.

"Whoa. That's . . . dark," I said.

My grandma had always been solidly Team Owen, even if she'd been sarcastic about it from time to time. The fact that she was coming at me so hard was jarring.

"I just can't believe this. You've gotten yourself into a lot of pickles over the years, but it was all . . . kid stuff. This is . . . this is serious, Owen," Mom said, her tone exhausted.

I hated that I'd drained her like that. "If I could take it back, I would. But the only thing I can do is try to make the best of it until we can get it all taken care of."

"So that's the answer, huh?" Mom accused. "Just let Vee's family throw some money at it and make it all just disappear? You took vows, Owen. You may have been drunk and upset, but that doesn't make them less binding."

I wanted to argue that it sure as shit should make them less binding. I was pretty sure in most places where the judge didn't have a God complex, it would absolutely be cause for a dissolution. Not that I wanted to deflect blame from myself, but the woman who'd married us clearly should've known we weren't in the right mind to enter into any kind of legal agreement. So what if we'd been annoying and persistent? She'd been derelict in her duty.

But Vee's uncle had said he'd handle it, and evidently his way didn't involve exposing the gross negligence of the officiant. I'd rocked the Diaz boat enough. It was time to stay steady and go with the flow.

I sighed. "What am I supposed to do, Mom? Stay married to Natalia while I'm in love with her cousin? Is that the right thing?"

"I don't think there is a right thing here, Owen."

I let the weight of her disappointment settle over me. "I need to bring her down to meet you."

"What?" Dad said.

"That's one of the judge's stipulations. I need to actually introduce her to my family. Unless you guys don't want that. I'm sure one white lie won't hurt." I couldn't help the hope that laced my voice.

"You want us to lie to a judge?" my mom asked, her voice dry enough to rival the Sahara.

"No," I rushed out. "You wouldn't have to lie. I'd just tell him you met her." Actually I'd try to convince Natalia to say it. She seemed better versed in lying.

"So you want to lie for us?"

I thought for a second. "I feel like I'm walking into a trap with no way out. I'm just trying to make this easier on you."

"Are you? Or are you just trying to make it easier on yourself?"

I sighed again. "When would it be convenient for us to come?"

"Whenever. We're not going anywhere."

"Okay. I'll check in with Natalia and get back to you."

"You do that."

"All right. I'll call you later, then," I said.

My mom hummed instead of replying, but just as I was about to disconnect, she said, "And, Owen? You bring *both* of your girls with you."

"Uh, I'm not sure that's a great idea. They both work, and coordinating my and Natalia's schedules is going to be hard enough. I don't think—"

"Oh, you thought I was asking? Work it out and let us know when you're coming." And with that, she hung up.

I stared at the phone for a long moment.

Well, shit.

Chapter Thirteen

OWEN

When I told the girls about visiting my parents, I was expecting more shock and dismay than I received. Natalia obviously knew that was going to have to happen, but I'd thought Vee would refuse to go. How awkward was it to meet the family of your potentially-soon-to-be-on-again boyfriend while he was married to your cousin? But Vee seemed not only willing to make the trip but also a little excited for it.

She said it was because she loved fireworks and there were bound to be a whole lot of them when we showed up. But it also seemed like there was more to it than that.

We were cleaning up after dinner—sans Natalia since she'd cooked—when I got the courage up to ask Vee about it.

"Do you really just want to go down to Virginia just to see me get yelled at by my parents?"

I hoped it wasn't only that. While I didn't begrudge her wanting to see me get mine, I also didn't want to take steps backward. And Vee wanting to see me berated for a mistake I was already clearly sorry for seemed like a huge step backward for us.

She smirked at me for a second, as if envisioning my parents giving me a hard time delighted her. But then she sobered. Dropping silverware into the sink, she turned and leaned against it so she was facing me.

"No, that's not the reason."

"Then what is?"

"It's silly."

"I doubt that."

She studied me for a moment. "I know that things are . . . weird right now. That we're in this awkward limbo, trying to figure out if we can make this work between us. But no guy has ever asked me to meet his parents before, and it's . . . a good feeling. Even though they're making you bring me, it still feels like a positive step."

I moved closer so that I could slide my arms around her. "The only reason I tried to argue with them about you coming was because I thought it would be uncomfortable for you. I want you to meet my parents very much. I just wish the circumstances were different."

"Me too. But they are what they are. Plus . . . it feels good to be working *through* our problems instead of trying to get around them. I don't want to avoid the hard stuff just because it's . . . hard."

"Me neither." I leaned in and pressed my lips against hers. We kept the kiss chaste, neither of us seeming to be ready to push for more too quickly.

After a minute, I took a step back but stayed within touching distance. "Speaking of not avoiding hard things, there's one other thing Natalia and I need to deal with."

"What?"

"Marriage counseling."

"Oh God. I forgot about that."

I groaned. "It's going to be brutal. The only positive is we have to do it over the computer, since it was mandated in Connecticut."

She smiled. "I'm surprised the judge isn't making you drive back up there for appointments."

I pressed a finger against her lips. "Shh. Don't speak it into existence."

She laughed and then turned back to the sink, running water over the silverware before putting them into the dishwasher. Minnie hadn't updated much in the house when she'd had it, but thankfully she'd at least installed one of those. Washing dishes was one of my least favorite chores.

"What do you have to do to make an appointment?" Vee asked.

"I have the number to call. I just need to . . . do it."

"No time like the present."

"You think there will still be someone there?" I glanced at the clock on the wall. Six thirty.

She shrugged. "I feel like they'd have to have evening hours for people who work. But there's only one way to find out for sure. Either way, I'm sure there's a way to leave a message."

"Yeah. I'll just run up and ask Natalia when works for her."

Vee offered me a small smile instead of a verbal reply.

I took the stairs two at a time and knocked on Natalia's door. She opened it wearing large headphones and white gunk all over her face.

"What's up?" she asked.

I shoved my hands in my pockets. "I was thinking we should call and make an appointment for the marriage counseling."

"Oh yeah. I forgot all about that."

Shocker.

"Yeah, I just wanted to check when worked best for you before I called."

"I'm working until four all week. So if they have anything after that, that'd be best. If not, I'm sure I can work something out. Nate's pretty easygoing."

I nodded. "I'll give them a call now and let you know."

"Thanks." She smiled widely as she closed the door, and I turned away, a tiny bit miffed she hadn't offered to make the call or at least call with me. I didn't mind doing the heavy lifting, but I also wasn't the only one who wanted this marriage annulled.

I went to my room, found the card we'd been given, and dialed the number.

"Thank you for calling Dr. Mulvaney's office. This is Jessica. How may I help you?"

Taken slightly aback, since I hadn't expected anyone to answer, it took me a second to respond.

"Uh, yes, hi, I, uh, I need to make an appointment for marriage counseling. Judge Kline told me to call." Shit, did mentioning the judge make me sound like a criminal? Or some kind of…bad husband or something? Maybe she'd just think I knew the judge and had asked him for a personal recommendation.

"Okay, so this is court mandated, then?"

Or maybe not. "Yes." I resisted the urge to tell her the entire story so she wouldn't think badly of me but realized that might also make me sound crazy in addition to everything else. The less said the better.

Rationally I knew I shouldn't even care. She was a

receptionist, not the counselor. And I'd have to come clean to the counselor anyway, so who cared?

I did apparently.

She asked me a bunch of questions and then set about finding us an available appointment. "Dr. Mulvaney is pretty booked, but she does have an opening in half an hour. We had a late cancellation. Would that work?"

My eyes widened in panic. No, that would *not* work. I had only mentally prepared myself to make the appointment. I was going to need more of a pep talk if I was going to actually participate in it. No, I was absolutely not ready to do this today.

"Sure, that works."

Damn me and my people pleasing!

"Great. I'll send you a link for your virtual session to the email you gave me."

"Thank you."

We disconnected, and I gave myself five minutes to freak out. When I was calm—or as calm as I was going to get—I went and knocked on Natalia's door. When she answered, I noticed she'd added some kind of black stuff on top of the white.

"Hey, they had an opening, so our meeting is in"—I looked down at my phone—"about twenty minutes."

Her eyes widened. "Twenty minutes! I need to keep this mask on for two hours."

"I doubt she'll care what you look like."

She rolled her eyes. "But I care what I look like. I don't want this person to think I'm crazy." She pushed past me and headed toward the bathroom.

It was on the tip of my tongue to say it didn't matter what this woman thought, but since I'd just had a mild panic attack not five minutes before, I knew I didn't have room to talk.

"I'll set up in the living room," I yelled before grabbing my laptop and heading downstairs.

"What are you up to?" Vee asked when she came into the living room and saw me setting up my laptop on the coffee table, positioning it so both Natalia and I would be in the frame when we sat on the couch.

"There was a cancellation, so our first counseling session is in a few minutes."

"Wow, that's intense."

"Yeah."

"Can I eavesdrop on it?" she asked, a wide smile on her face.

I reached back and grabbed my neck. "I'm not sure how to answer that."

"Why not?" She looked confused.

"I don't want you to think I have something to hide, but I also don't know that I can survive this with an audience. I'm super nervous." I held up a hand when I saw she was about to speak. "Which I know doesn't make any sense. We're just jumping through the hoops the judge forced on us. But I've never spoken to any kind of therapist before, and it's making me feel like I might hyperventilate."

Vee came and sat beside me on the couch, putting her hand on my leg, which I was sure she thought was reassuring but only served to make me more flustered. Though maybe thinking about where else I wished she'd put her hand would distract me from the session.

Maybe the counselor could help me stop being such a perv.

"I think it's normal to be nervous," Vee said sweetly. "This is a new experience, and the circumstances are . . . odd. But I'm sure it'll be fine."

"I know you're right." I let out a long breath. "It's not like we actually have to impress this person. We only need her to sign off that we had the sessions."

"How many sessions do you need to do?"

My brow furrowed. "The judge didn't actually say, and I didn't even think to ask. Shit, I guess I'll have to get in touch with him again to find out."

Vee offered me a sympathetic smile, and I got lost in looking at her for a bit before Natalia blew into the room.

"Okay, I'm ready. Let's do the damn thing." Her face was washed clean of whatever the hell had been on it, her makeup reapplied, and her hair done. "You joining us?" she asked Vee, her question sounding genuine.

"Nah, I'll leave you two to it." Vee gave my leg a pat before standing and heading out of the room.

"I'll come up after and tell you all about it," Natalia said.

"You better," Vee called over her shoulder as she disappeared from view.

Natalia took Vee's vacated seat beside me. "Okay, so how are we playing this?"

"Playing it?"

"Yeah, are we going to pretend we're a happy couple or like we're actively plotting each other's murder? Something in between?"

"I thought we'd just go with the truth," I said, though my voice rose at the end, making it sound like a question.

Her face fell. "Oh. That's boring."

"She has to report back to the judge, so I don't think lying is the best idea."

"Man, that guy takes the fun out of everything," she muttered.

I had to agree.

VERONICA

I played around on my phone while I waited for Owen and Nattie to finish with their session. I had to admit, I was disappointed Owen hadn't wanted me to listen, mostly because I was curious what the counselor would ask and how Natalia would answer. That girl was a wild card if ever there was one.

To occupy my time, I sent some texts to my dad and brothers to check in and then scrolled through social media. I fell down a rabbit hole of a woman who owned a farm with a bunch of animals who seemed to be plotting to kill her.

A knock on my door broke my trance, and when I looked at the time, I saw an hour had passed. Climbing off my bed, I pulled open the door to see Owen and Nattie both standing there.

"How'd it go?" I asked.

"Evidently Owen and I were supposed to contact her immediately after meeting Judge Doom," Nattie said. "I guess his office sent paperwork saying we had to meet with her once a week for the whole three months we're 'together.' We told her he hadn't told us that, but it didn't look like she believed us. She was pretty judgy for a counselor. Zero stars. Do not recommend."

I looked to Owen for his take.

He rolled his eyes behind Nattie's head. "You just don't like her because she didn't know who Amy Adams was."

"No, I don't like her because when someone compliments you by saying you resemble a famous actress, you should say thank you regardless of whether you know who they are or not. It's called common courtesy. Sticking your nose up like you're too good to watch movies or know about pop culture isn't a good look."

"If she didn't know her, she probably didn't know for sure it was a compliment," I reasoned.

"She knew. I used my genuine smile when I said it."

"You have different smiles?" Owen asked.

"Of course. Everybody does."

Owen seemed to think that over before saying, "I guess."

"I'm not sure people use them as a weapon quite like you do," I added.

Nattie shrugged. "Their mistake."

"So do you have to make up all the sessions?" I asked to get us back on track.

"She said weekly meetings from here on out would be enough as long as we seemed committed to the plan," Owen said on a sigh. "I don't even know what that means. Committed to the plan to get our marriage annulled? Because that's my plan."

"Why didn't you ask her?" I said.

Owen gave me a skeptical look. "She was kind of... intimidating."

Nattie hummed. "She definitely seemed invested in us staying together. Made us say all the things we liked about each other and asked us to visualize the future if we stayed together. I said it looked bleak because my cousin would probably hire a hitman to take me out. She didn't seem sure of how to respond to that."

"That's...understandable," I said. "Talking about hired hits while in a marriage counseling session is probably a major red flag."

Nattie waved me off. "It's not like I said Owen and I would kill each other. That should've made her feel better. But since she has a major stick up her butt, she probably never feels good." She tilted her head and looked at the ceiling. "Unless she's into that sort of thing."

"Having a stick up her butt?" I asked.

"Don't shame. People are into that. But judging from her overall demeanor, she probably doesn't find willing partners all that often. Even if she looks like Amy Adams."

I wanted to point out that Nattie was doing a lot of judging for someone who just accused her therapist of the same thing, but really, what was the point? "I wasn't shaming anyone. Just...looking for clarification."

"Anyway," Owen said, seeming a little uncomfortable with the direction the conversation had taken. "She fit us into her schedule every Wednesday at six."

"And she acted like a real martyr for doing it," Nattie said. "Said that's usually her night to play pumpkin patch or whatever, but she'd push it back just for us."

"It was squash," Owen corrected.

Nattie rolled her eyes and flapped her hand in a *whatever* gesture. "Wednesday used to be my favorite day of the week, and now she's ruined it."

My face contorted in confusion. "Why would Wednesday be your favorite night of the week?"

"It's the night I give myself a mini spa session. I used to go to Apple Plum Spa every week, but my dad said he'd disown me if I spent any more money there. So I started doing it at home, which isn't nearly as fun, but what can ya do, right?"

Owen mouthed *Apple Plum?* at me.

I gave him a quick shrug before telling Nattie, "Makes sense," though it didn't really.

"Can't you switch your spa routine to a different night?" Owen asked.

She glared at him. "I'm only willing to give up so much for this marriage, Owen."

Guess we'd finally found her line in the sand. Uprooting her whole life to move down here was evidently nothing in the face of interrupting her beauty routine.

"I'm going to go try to salvage the rest of my face masks," she said.

"You use multiple face masks?" I asked. "At once?"

She looked at me with pity before rubbing the back of her index finger down my cheek. "It makes so much sense now," she whispered as if she were speaking to herself.

Was this bitch talking shit about my skin? I opened my mouth to ask her, but she'd already started for her own room, and Owen, likely seeing the murderous intent on my face, gently pushed me back and closed my bedroom door behind him.

I walked over to my mirror and inspected my face.

"You can't seriously think there's anything wrong with your skin," Owen said. "You're gorgeous. And you don't need a face mask to be that way."

"I do use face masks sometimes. But not seventy at once like she does."

"There's no way putting all that goop on her face can be good for her pores," Owen reasoned.

And even though Nattie had pretty flawless skin, I let his

words soothe me. I walked over to him and wrapped my arms around his waist, leaning my side of my head against his chest.

"Thank you. I know I'm being silly."

He squeezed me to him. "Not silly. Just . . . unnecessarily worried."

"You're very sweet to me," I said. He was probably sweeter than I deserved.

"It's not a hardship." He chuckled, the movement causing my head to jostle a bit, though the rhythmic quality of it was kind of soothing. I liked happy Owen.

We stood there for a bit, soaking up each other's warmth and rocking slightly, almost like we were dancing to music only we could hear.

I wished we could stay in this bubble where being close to each other like this was enough. But the real world always came calling.

Chapter Fourteen

OWEN

A vibration in my front pocket jolted me out of the moment with Vee.

She sighed, pulling back to give me space to retrieve my phone.

Brody's name was on the screen.

"Hey."

"Hey. I have a favor to ask."

"What?" I asked cautiously. A Brody favor could be anything from wanting to borrow a hoodie to asking us to try to ship him to Thailand in a packaging crate.

"I need your kitchen."

"My kitchen? Why?"

"Do you have any idea how much wedding cakes are? Or at least how much the ones Aamee wants are?"

"No. But aren't her parents paying for most of the wedding anyway?" I put the phone on speaker because a good boyfriend—or hopefully soon-to-be boyfriend; we really needed to talk about labels—wouldn't withhold whatever nonsense this was going to turn into.

"Yeah, but they're still kind of salty about Aamee quitting working for her mom, so they're only giving us a set amount and told Aamee they wouldn't give her a dime more. Don't get me wrong, they still gave us a fuck-ton of money. But I'm trying to convince Aamee to cut a few corners so we can save some of that money for other things rather than blowing it all on the wedding."

That level of forethought from Brody was . . . surprising. "That's a good way to think," I told him. "I'm sure that money would go a long way to helping you guys get started on your life together."

"I know, right? Like, who wouldn't want a hot tub to hang out in or a basketball court in their backyard? There are so many more important things we could be using it for."

And there it was. "Yeah, or for a down payment on a house so you have somewhere to put those things."

"Eh, yeah, I guess. Whatever. So anyway, can I?"

"Can you what?"

"Use your kitchen to show Aamee I can make our wedding cake."

"Oh, um . . ." I looked at Vee, who was nodding her head with vigor. I watched her pull out her own phone and begin tapping away on it. "Sure. When did you wanna come over?"

"Tomorrow? I have to find a recipe and buy the stuff I need, but then I'll be ready to go."

"Yeah, that works. Maybe we can order pizza while you . . . bake."

"Perfect. Thanks, man. I really appreciate it."

"No problem."

I hung up and looked at Vee. "He's going to destroy my kitchen, isn't he?"

"Absolutely," she replied, still pecking away at her screen.

"What are you writing?"

"I'm texting everyone that they better get over here tomorrow. This is going to be too epic to miss."

"Shouldn't we have asked Brody if he wanted everyone to come over?"

She looked up at me. "Do you think Brody would've stopped to ask that if the roles were reversed?"

"Good point. Carry on."

She smiled a diabolical little smile that was too cute for words. Natalia was right. We all did have different kinds.

VERONICA

It had taken approximately eight minutes for Brody to destroy our kitchen. Honestly, I was a little surprised it had taken him that long, but he wasted a good bit of that time staring helplessly at the ingredients in front of him.

As soon as he opened the flour, it was all over.

I'd expected him to buy boxed cake mix, but I was wrong again. Seemed Brody was out to prove himself because he was starting from scratch.

Almost the entire crew, sans Natalia, who said she'd had something to do, and Carter and Toby, who'd said they'd be here but weren't yet, had gathered to watch the Brody spectacle, and he had our rapt attention. We stood silently as we watched him struggle to read the recipe and connect it with an appropriate action.

"You guys are making me nervous. Don't you have something else to do?" Brody asked, sounding exasperated.

"Watching you is literally what we all came here for," his sister, Sophia, replied.

Brody's eyes flashed around at all of us before they settled on Drew's brother. "You even called Cody?"

Drew looked over at his brother before turning his attention back to Brody and shrugging. "We needed someone to film."

Cody had brought his GoPro and had it fixed on Brody as he wandered around the kitchen as if he expected the appliances to tell him what to do.

"This had better not end up on the internet," Brody warned, wielding a spatula and shaking it in Cody's direction.

"Where else am I supposed to put it?" Cody asked.

"I hate all of you," Brody muttered, causing Aamee to squawk.

"Hey!"

"Not you, love buns," Brody said.

Ransom drifted toward Owen. "You have a fire extinguisher around?"

"Yeah, three. I bought an extra one this morning. Two are in the pantry and another is under the sink."

"Good planning."

Owen nodded sagely.

Brody mumbled to himself as he set out the things he thought he'd need, then rearranged them, then arranged them again. The dry ingredients he'd already opened caused a smokelike plume of powder to erupt every time he moved them.

"There's no more weed butter in there, is there?" I whispered to Owen.

"Sadly, no," he replied.

Brody continued to fidget with the materials before him.

"You gonna combine any of that stuff anytime soon, or just hope it eventually does it itself?" Drew asked Brody.

Brody flipped him off without looking up, his eyes fixed on the counter.

Suddenly, I heard the front door fly open and slam closed again before heavy feet sounded against the floors. "Did we miss it?" Carter asked, out of breath as he ran into the kitchen.

"Miss what?" Brody asked.

Carter gestured toward Brody. "Whatever you're gonna do to this kitchen."

Toby entered at a more sedate pace. "Hey, everyone. Where's Gimli?" he asked Owen.

"I put him in my room in case of ... something," Owen replied.

"Do you think that's a good idea?" Carter wondered. "It might be tough to get up there if there's a fire."

"For fuck's sake, there's not going to be a fire," Brody yelled. "I've cooked and baked before. Tell them, Soph."

Sophia looked perplexed. "I have no recollection of this."

"In ninth grade when I ran for class president. I baked all those cookies to give out for votes."

"You didn't bake those," Sophia said, her voice sounding incredulous. "They were Chips Ahoy Mom bought from the store."

Brody pointed his finger at her. "You're a lying liar who lies. It took me hours to bake all those cookies. Mom finally took pity on me and finished them up while I went to bed."

"Brody, they were little hockey pucks. She threw them all out and went to the store and bought you cookies to hand out. They were even still in the original container."

Now it was Brody's turn to look confused. "I thought she just wrapped them in that so they'd stay fresh."

"They were still sealed."

"I don't know how cookie packaging works, Sophia."

Sophia rubbed her eyes with her fingers. "You're the reason there are directions on shampoo."

Brody looked around at all the ingredients set out before him, and then looked back at Sophia. "She really bought them?" He looked disappointed, and it made my heart pang for him. Poor, stupid Brody.

Sophia nodded.

He sighed. "My whole life is a lie."

"No more of a lie than it was when you paid Drew to be you for a semester," Taylor offered, her voice upbeat like she was contributing something helpful.

"Brody," Aamee broke in as she looked around at all of us. "No offense, but I don't want to hang out here all night. It literally feels like I hang out with no one besides you people."

"With a sunny disposition like that, I'm sure you have people banging down your crypt to hang out with you," Sophia said, a phony smile spread across her face.

Aamee gave her a saccharine look in response before her face morphed back to its normal, bitchy state.

Brody was quiet for a moment before he said, "I can do this. I can avenge my cookies."

"Gotta say," Carter interjected, munching on a bag of chips he must've stolen out of the pantry, "I thought this would be more entertaining."

"Yeah, my videographer skills are being wasted," Cody agreed.

The doorbell chimed, and Owen announced, "Pizza's here."

"I'll get it," Carter called as he booked it toward the front door. That guy was always hungry.

Brody walked toward us, arms outstretched like he was herding cats. "You guys go eat the pizza in the living room, and I'll stay here and bake dessert."

"Without supervision?" Owen asked, clearly worried about his kitchen.

"I'll stay," Aamee offered.

"No, I want it to be a surprise," Brody said. "And honestly, you make me a little nervous sometimes."

Aamee looked flattered by that.

"I can stay," I offered. Brody and I had grown close when we'd had to pretend to be married, so I figured that out of everyone left—barring maybe Drew—I was the least likely to give him anxiety.

"Yeah, okay, Vee can stay. But everyone else has gotta go."

Everyone headed out but Owen. "You want me to bring you some food?" he asked like the sweet, doting man he was.

"That'd be great."

He smiled before following the gang out of the room.

I slipped into a chair and looked at Brody. "So what are you gonna do?"

His brow was set in determination. "I'm gonna make a cake."

"Aamee is never going to let you bake your wedding cake. You have to know this."

Brody shook his head. "She promised that if it was presentable and tasted good, I could."

"Why do you even want the stress? You're going to have so many other things to worry about."

He shrugged. "I like being difficult."

I snorted. "Who didn't know that?"

"Seriously, though. How mad is she going to be if this cake is decent? It's going to be epic."

"There's just one problem with that scenario."

"What?"

I stared at him in amazement. "You can't bake."

"How do you *know* that? I haven't even tried since ninth grade."

"Educated guess," I answered.

"You'll see," he said, the words sounding like a warning. Then he set to work, and I settled in to watch. Owen brought me food and a soda, continuing to check on me here and there, but Brody always shooed him out. Brody said Owen was distracting him from his process.

The only process I could discern was that Brody seemed intent on using every available surface, bowl, and utensil in the kitchen while he baked. He better have been planning on cleaning this shit up.

I had to admit, I hadn't been expecting him to get one cake in the oven, let alone three. But in they all went, looking only marginally lumpy. One also was a weird blue color Brody said used his "secret ingredient." I hoped it wasn't laundry detergent or something. I hadn't seen a bottle of Tide, but I hadn't seen anything else that could be considered a secret ingredient either.

Guess we'd find out.

While he waited for the cakes to bake, he started making the frosting, which was a nightmare if I'd ever seen one. Owen and I would probably be finding sticky remnants of it for months.

Finally, after what seemed like an eternity, Brody pulled

the cakes out and looked like he was about to frost them. I'd remained mostly quiet, but I didn't want him to fail this close to the finish line.

"They need to cool first," I said. "If you frost them right away, the frosting will melt and drip off."

Brody looked up at me as if he were just remembering I was there. "Oh." He looked at the clock on the microwave. "It's already been a while. Can I somehow cool them faster?"

"Maybe put them in the freezer for a few minutes? They do that sometimes on those baking shows."

He thought for a second and then nodded decisively. "Yeah, that's a good idea."

It really might not have been, since I had no real baking knowledge either, but whatever. I doubted it would ruin them. At least no more than they already were, having been made by Brody.

Once Brody had dealt with the cakes, he put his hands on the counter and leaned on them, staring straight at me.

"What?" I asked.

"What's going on with my favorite throuple?"

"Gross. Please don't ever call us that again."

He smiled but didn't say more, obviously hoping I'd cave under his penetrative stare.

Which I did. "Ugh, I don't know." I rubbed my face with my hands. "Owen and I are . . . taking things slow."

"But there are *things* to be taking slowly?"

"Yeah. Not any major things. But we're spending time together. Trying to get back on track."

"That's good."

"Is it?" I asked, genuinely curious about what he thought. Despite Brody's airhead persona, he wasn't stupid.

He took a second before answering, which I appreciated. Brody wouldn't give empty platitudes. If I asked his opinion, I was going to get it—whether I'd like what he had to say or not.

"I think so, yeah. Owen's a good guy. The whole marrying your cousin thing... that's not him, ya know? Call it a night of insanity or whatever. Because there's no denying he's sprung on you. We can all see it. And you deserve someone who looks at you the way Owen does."

I took a deep breath as if inhaling his words. "I worry this is all a giant red flag and my feelings for him are making me ignore it."

He looked down at the counter as he seemed to chew on what I'd said before returning his gaze to me. "I've hung out with all kinds of guys. Frat boys, entitled rich guys, troublemakers, slackers, all of 'em. Hell, I've *been* almost all of them. I can spot a scumbag from a mile away." The look on his face was as serious as I'd ever seen on him. "Owen isn't any of those guys. And deep down, when you dig past your insecurities, I think you know that."

I took a shuddering breath as my throat tightened and tears prickled my eyes. I didn't know why I was getting emotional. Maybe because it was validating, having Brody back up my instincts. I'd felt so betrayed by both Owen and Nattie and was worried my family would judge my giving them a second chance that I'd doubted what I knew in my heart.

Owen had hurt me, but he hadn't done it on purpose. He was a young guy who had made a mistake—one he was clearly sorry for. And he was working to fix it. I had to let go of what other people would think and focus on what I knew. Owen and I were good together, *happy* together. Giving him a second chance didn't mean I was naïve and stupid. It meant I was human and I was in love. I wouldn't rush us, but I was open to whatever came next.

In truth, I knew I already had been. Kissing and hanging out more with Owen had put that in motion already. But I felt better about it after my talk with Brody. More confident in the decision.

We chatted about how the wedding planning was going, Brody's attempts to thwart Aamee from devolving into full Bridezilla mode, and if I was excited for law school in the fall. Brody eventually decided the cakes were cool enough and set about frosting and decorating them. He even pulled a bride and groom cake topper out of a bag and set it on top, slightly askew but cute nonetheless.

I had to admit, I was impressed. The cake was clearly the work of an amateur, but it looked edible. Of course, looks could be deceiving. But he hadn't caused any major catastrophes, which was a decided win. At least from his perspective. Those of us who'd gathered for that exact reason were going to be disappointed.

We got some plates and utensils before Brody picked up the cake and carried it out to where everyone was gathered in the living room.

"Oh shit, he actually made a cake," I heard Ransom say.

"What did you think I was doing? Ironing?" Brody asked.

"Well, I for one expected the cakes to be flat, so I wasn't dismissing ironing," Sophia snarked.

"Eat the cake," Brody quipped as he set it down on the coffee table. "I'm not sure if I hope it's good or kills all of you."

"If anyone could manage both, it'd be you," Sophia replied.

Brody moved to cut into it, but Carter thrust a hand out to stop him. "Wait. We haven't evaluated you on presentation yet." Carter stood and slowly made his way around the cake, his hand cupping his chin as if he was considering it closely. "How do you feel about the penises, Aamee?" he asked.

"Those are flowers," Brody growled.

Carter's face screwed up. "You probably should've left that open to interpretation. I've become quite partial to penises myself." He shot a wink at Toby. "Flowers? Not so much."

I tilted my head as I looked at the cake. Brody had used various colors of icing to decorate the cake, and since he'd narrated what he was doing as he worked, I knew what they were supposed to be. But now that Carter had mentioned it, they did look a little like multicolored penises.

"Is the top layer leaning?" Taylor asked.

"I think it's actually the bottom layer that's uneven, making the whole thing have Tower of Pisa vibes," Ransom replied.

Brody rolled his eyes. "You guys don't even matter. What do you think, Aamee?"

We all turned our attention to Aamee, expecting her typical, acerbic reply. But she wasn't even looking at the cake. Her gaze was on Brody, and her normally bitchy glare softened.

"Since I'm partial to both penises and flowers, I think the cake is . . . interesting. I like that it's open to interpretation."

That was one way of putting it.

"And asymmetrical cakes are really popular right now, so the fact that it's a little lopsided makes it trendy," she added.

"Asymmetrical cakes?" Cody asked. "That's a thing?"

"Apparently," Drew replied.

"Okay, solid marks from Aamee," Carter said. "I'm guessing that has a lot to do with the fact she has sex with you, but whatever. Let's cut into that sucker."

Brody rolled his eyes but picked up the knife to start cutting slices. Since I was still standing beside him, I held up plates for him and then passed them around. The top tier was the weird blue one, and it looked like he was hacking into a Smurf, but the cake appeared fluffy otherwise.

When each of us had a slice, we all looked at each other, forks poised as if none of us wanted to be the first to try it. By silent agreement, we all scooped up a sliver and ate it, chewing slowly as if prepared to go into cardiac arrest at any moment. After swallowing, we all exchanged looks again.

Finally, Owen spoke. "It's . . . good." He said it as if it were a question, almost as if he wasn't sure he was allowed to express his satisfaction.

"Good might be a stretch," Taylor added as she took another bite. "But it's definitely not bad."

"It's kind of . . . tangy," Drew said. "I can't tell if I like it or not."

We all forked some more into our mouths as we tried to come to a conclusion about the cake.

"What did you put in it to make it blue?" Toby asked.

"Food coloring," Brody replied.

"What flavor is it?" Cody questioned.

"I swiped some sour mix from the bar and added that in. Thought it might give it a little something."

"I . . . hate that I don't hate it," Sophia said.

"Maybe we should try the other layers too," Cody suggested, eyeing the cake hungrily.

We all nodded our agreement and accepted more cake as Brody cut it. The second layer was regular vanilla and a little dry, but still edible.

"Well?" Brody asked, looking at Aamee.

She sighed and set her plate down. "What if we compromise?"

Brody looked wary. "Compromise how?"

"I'll promise to downsize the cake so the price is more reasonable, and you can bake your own groom's cake."

Brody thought it over for a minute before sticking his hand out toward her. "Deal."

With that settled, Taylor turned to me. "I hear you're going down to see Jimi. I'm so jealous. She's great. But a word of warning, don't play any card games with them. They're merciless."

At my quizzical look, Ransom added, "They got her so drunk she started talking to their chickens."

I nodded like that made total sense. "Thanks for the heads-up."

Even though I knew Taylor and Ransom had met Owen's family, it still made me a bit disappointed that I wouldn't be the first person he took home who was part of his life up here. Which I knew was silly, but it was what it was.

Owen knocked his shoulder against mine. "They're going to love you."

I smiled, really hoping that was true.

Chapter Fifteen

VERONICA

I didn't know what I thought the ride to Virginia to visit Owen's family would be like, but I wasn't prepared to be stuck in his truck with Nattie and Adrien arguing in the back seat while I held Gimli on my lap to prevent him from trying to climb out the window that Owen insisted we keep open because of Gimli's claustrophobia.

We'd stopped at a rest stop a little while ago, and Owen had given us all a "tour" of the spot he'd found Gimli when he'd hitched a ride home with Taylor and Ransom back in the fall. Gimli actually seemed to remember the place, and I wondered if he'd simply gotten lost from his home nearby only to be "rescued" by Owen. Though I'd never suggest that possibility aloud because Owen would probably spend most of the day searching for Gimli's owners to be sure he hadn't taken the animal unethically.

Hoping to pretend I was anywhere but here, I turned up the music on my phone and changed my AirPod setting to cancel environmental noise. Why Nattie had insisted on bringing someone along to Virginia made absolutely no sense. And why she chose her pain-in-the-ass older brother, Adrien, made even less sense.

She'd claimed she would feel like a third wheel if it was just the three of us, and despite my arguing that she and Owen were a couple—technically speaking—she put up enough of a fight about it that I eventually agreed to a fourth person just so I didn't have to hear her complain.

"Are we there yet?" Adrien whined. "I've had to pee ever since we left that gas station."

Apparently my headphones didn't cancel as much noise as they claimed because I could still hear the voices behind me.

"Why didn't you pee *at* the rest stop?"

"I didn't have to go then. I said I've had to pee *since* then."

"We've got another forty-five minutes or so," Owen told him. "But I can stop again if you want."

"He can hold it," I said. "It's his fault he didn't go when we stopped."

"Just because it's my fault doesn't mean I have to go any less."

"I'll pull over." Owen began to slow down and put on his turn signal.

"It's not safe for him to get out on the side of the highway," I argued. "He'll need to hold it."

"It's dangerous for all of us if we *don't* pull over. All I have to pee in is this empty Monster can. I don't even have a bottle." Adrien leaned forward and put his hand on Owen's shoulder as he pleaded with him. "Bro, would you really let another dude stick his dick in a can?"

"You're disgusting," Nattie and I both said at almost the exact same time. At least we could agree on something.

"Dude, don't stick it *in* the can," Owen warned.

"Well, obviously not fully in," Adrien said. "I'm not small. But the tip's gotta match up with the opening, and that's a risk I don't wanna take."

"Then just wait till we get there," I said again. "You'll survive."

Owen kept driving while Adrien squirmed and whined in the back seat like a child. By the time we pulled into the driveway that led to a large yellow house, Adrien leaped out of the truck and ran toward the front door. I didn't even wonder if he was going to just let himself in because I already knew the answer. Adrien's etiquette needed serious work. The rest of us climbed out of the truck, and I put Gimli down in the grass.

The three of us stretched, and then Owen pulled our bags out of the bed of his truck. We began walking up to the porch when the storm door opened and Adrien reversed out of it with his hands up. He stumbled as he attempted to back up quickly down the wood steps.

"I'm with Owen," he said, his voice shaking. "I'm a friend of Owen's." He turned toward us. "See?"

I wasn't sure what exactly was happening, but I wasn't exactly sad to see an old woman pointing a shotgun at my cousin.

"He with you?" she called to Owen.

And without missing a beat, Owen said, "Never seen him before in my life, Grandma."

"Then get the hell off my property before it becomes your eternal resting place," the woman warned.

"You must be Jimi," I said, walking toward where Adrien was already down on his knees with his hands behind his head like he was about to get arrested. "You've been on the wrong side of the law way too many times," I said to him as I walked by.

Then I looked back at the gray-haired woman holding the gun. "I'm Vee. I've heard so much about you."

"Believin' nasty rumors about someone you've never met's akin to spreading 'em around yourself," she said, keeping the shotgun pointed at Adrien.

"Oh no," I said, smiling. I loved her already. "I didn't hear anything nasty about you. All good. Taylor and Ransom would never say anything negative about someone, especially someone's grandmother."

"Oh, I know those two would never say a bad word about somebody. They're sweet as pie. I was talkin' about my grandson over there. He's got some loose lips, that one."

I couldn't argue with that, so I just laughed. "Nice to meet you, Jimi," I said. "May I call you that?"

"No, you certainly may not. You'll call me Grandma just like all my grandkids."

I assumed that at some point Owen had told Jimi we were together, but I'd also assumed that since he'd brought his current wife with him, he also would've shared that we'd since broken up.

"I told you we're not together anymore though," Owen began before Jimi cut him off.

"Hush up before I point this your way instead."

"Come on," Owen said, walking toward the front porch with a bag in each hand and one on his back. "You know I know that thing's not loaded. Hasn't even been shot in a decade, I bet."

"Told you he blabs," she said to me.

Jimi ordered Adrien to stand up, and then she lowered

the gun. "That was fun," she said. "Bathroom's down the hall before you get to the kitchen."

I wondered if Adrien had already pissed himself. For a guy who'd spent more than a little time in jail, he seemed scared shitless. I watched him run up the steps and into the house, and once he was inside, we all laughed loudly.

"I like you, Grandma," Nattie said, adjusting her sequined bag on her shoulder.

"You can call me Jimi," she said before turning toward the house and waving us in with her shotgun.

I'd never felt so welcomed by a stranger in my life.

OWEN

I never thought this trip would go smoothly, but I also wasn't prepared for how intensely awkward it would be for everyone involved. I wasn't aware that I had any sort of vision for what it would be like for my wife to meet my family, but as I introduced Natalia, it became clear that this wasn't it.

For starters, I always thought my wife wouldn't be my *wife* until after my family had a chance to meet her. We'd spend time together, she'd spend time with my family, and everyone would grow to love her as much as I did. Instead, I had a girl I barely knew, my immature brother-in-law, and my ex-girlfriend standing beside me in my parents' living room.

"I know this isn't . . . ideal," I said after my mom gave Vee and Natalia polite hugs. Then she turned to Adrien.

"Bring it in, Mrs. Parrish," he said, his arms outstretched for a moment before he wrapped them around her petite body and pulled her into a strong embrace.

"All right, that's enough," my dad said. Both he and my grandfather were large men—tall, solid, intimidating if they wanted to be. And right now, I could see my dad wanted to be.

Adrien let go of my mom, and she smoothed over the wrinkles in her white shirt.

"Who wants some sweet tea?" she asked before disappearing into the kitchen without waiting for anyone to answer.

"I'm gonna go help Claudette with lunch," my dad said. "Why don't y'all get yourselves settled in the meantime? Owen, can you show your friends where they're staying?"

"Oh, um, where *is* everyone staying?" Too preoccupied with other, more important things, like how I was going to get through the next few days, I hadn't even thought about the sleeping arrangements.

"Well, we don't have much extra space," my dad said to the others. "My parents use one of the spare bedrooms, but there is one other bedroom in addition to Owen's. It has a double bed, like Owen's room, but I also set up an air mattress in there. I figured I'd leave it up to y'all to decide who's where."

I assumed that Adrien and Natalia had no interest in sharing a bed, and I knew better than to think that Vee would share a bed with Natalia. "I guess Natalia and Adrien can take the spare room since that has an extra mattress. Vee, you can take my bed. I'll sleep on the floor or down here on the couch if you want the room to yourself."

They followed me upstairs and put their bags in the rooms.

Natalia pushed her brother out almost immediately. "I have to get changed," she said once he was out of the room and she'd locked the door.

"Why?"

"Because I don't wear an outfit for more than six hours. You know that."

Adrien looked at me. "Dude, your wife's seriously high maintenance."

"Can you not call her that, please?"

"Well, that's why we're here. And don't you two have to do couple-y things while you're visiting? That's what Natalia told me."

"Not *couple-y* things," Vee said sternly. "The judge did say they need to spend some time together and she needs to meet Owen's family. But he didn't specify that it had to be just the two of them."

"Oh, got it," Adrien said. "Like a double date."

Vee's eyes narrowed like she was seeing a ghost and couldn't be sure whether her eyes were deceiving her. "No. Not like a double date. We're cousins."

"So?" Adrien said.

"So cousins don't date."

"Uh, they do in Virginia."

"That's offensive," Vee said. "And even if we weren't cousins, I'd *never* date you."

"Well, *that's* offensive," he said. I actually thought Adrien did look offended by that, albeit only slightly. Then he turned to me. "Sorry, bro. I was only kidding about the incest thing."

I wasn't sure if he'd actually been kidding or had really thought it and been embarrassed to admit it. Either way it didn't matter.

"It's all good," I told him. "Why don't we head down and see what's on the menu for lunch?"

"There's a menu we can order from?" Adrien asked excitedly.

"Seriously?" Vee said to him.

Adrien didn't respond, and for some reason, I almost felt bad for the guy. Almost.

I knocked on the door to the guest room and told Natalia we'd be downstairs whenever she was ready. Then the three of us headed down to have what would certainly be one of the most uncomfortable meals of my life.

Chapter Sixteen

VERONICA

Being at Owen's had put me on the offensive. I could tell I'd been snippy, but at least it had only been in front of my cousins and Owen. I didn't want his family to think I was some emotional bitch. I wanted them to like me. I wasn't going to put on a fake persona to make that happen; I wasn't that type of person. But I didn't want them to see the worst version of me either. And since this whole situation seemed to be putting me on the offensive, I'd have to be careful to keep it in check, even with my cousins who I had a naturally snippy relationship with at times.

"This is fantastic," I said to Owen's mom, Claudette, about the salad. I'd never tasted anything quite like it. It had roasted vegetables and feta and tasted like something that might be on a menu at a farm-to-table café somewhere.

Claudette smiled warmly. "The secret is shaved brussels sprouts."

Owen's dad, RJ, interjected. "Brussels sprouts are one of the worst vegetables, but somehow they work here."

"And the chicken's fresh from the yard," Jimi said. "He won the lottery today. Or lost, depending on how you look at it."

"Grandma," Owen said, giving her a look like he wished she'd be quiet but didn't actually want to say it.

I stopped chewing for a moment but managed to make myself swallow what was in my mouth before speaking.

"She's kidding, right?"

"Yes, of course she is," Owen said. "If you haven't noticed yet, she has a warped sense of humor that's only appealing to a select few."

I'd almost forgotten Natalia existed until I heard her voice from the other room. "You're telling me," she said. "That room is full of freaky-ass dolls. I'm not even sure I can sleep in there." She turned to Claudette. "No offense if you're into that stuff. I just . . . I felt like they were watching me get changed."

"No one wants to watch you get changed," I told her. I really needed to rein myself in, but it was so incredibly difficult when I was used to letting the snark fly.

Jimi let out a loud laugh. "Now that's funny," she said about my comment. "Take a seat, hon. There's room right here. Grab a plate."

Natalia did as Jimi said, and thankfully, the room was mostly quiet except for the sounds of utensils scraping plates and the awkward sound of people chewing.

"You'll get used to the dolls," Claudette said. "I'm not much of a fan either, but Jimi has some sort of odd attachment to those things."

"They're gonna be worth money someday, and when I die, you'll be happy."

Claudette smiled at her. "I can't argue with that part."

Owen's grandfather, Roland, laughed loudly at that. The jabs this family threw at each other helped me loosen up a little. They reminded me a little of my own family that way.

We all continued to dig in, passing the cornbread and ham and little sandwiches on those Hawaiian rolls. Somehow the sweetness of the dough made it easy to eat way more than I would've normally.

"So what do y'all have planned for the rest of the day?" RJ asked.

Owen looked to me, though I had no idea why. It wasn't like I knew what was around here or was in any way prepared to plan something for us. I hadn't exactly envisioned this trip as a vacation chock-full of fun-filled activities. I was basically here because there was no way in hell I was gonna let Owen and Natalia visit his parents without witnessing the whole thing. It was a form of self-harm even an emo teenager would be envious of.

"We have to do things we can take pictures of," Nattie interjected.

"Pictures?" Owen's grandfather raised an eyebrow, and Owen hung his head before breathing in deeply and preparing to answer.

"Yeah. The judge wants proof we tried to make the marriage work and actually spent time together."

"Ha!" Jimi laughed more loudly than was natural. "This is crazy, even for you," she said to Owen. "But I volunteer to take the pictures. No way I'm missing this disaster."

"I'm glad my suffering provides you with so much pleasure."

Jimi smiled widely. "Me too."

OWEN

I was prepared for a hazing from my family, so it didn't surprise me when I got one during the first meal we all shared together. They spent the rest of the lunch brainstorming ideas for photo ops, including feeding the chickens, horseback riding, picking wild flowers in the field, and making breakfast together.

I drew the line at feeding each other dessert when my dad suggested it. And even though I knew he was only joking to get a rise out of me, the thought actually sickened me to think about.

Nattie wasn't disgusting by any means, and objectively speaking, she was very attractive. But doing something so intimate, especially with Vee right there to witness it, made me feel queasy.

"All right, all right," my mom said as we were finishing up lunch. "Let's give them a break. I'm sure they don't need this to be any worse than it'll already be."

"Oooh, a break. That's a good idea," my grandma said. "Owen, what if we pretended you broke your leg or something and we had Natalia take care of you?"

I glared at her from across the table. "Speaking of breaks, you better watch it, or you might find yourself with a broken hip again, old woman."

"Owen Worthington Parrish, are you threatening your grandmother?"

"I'd never," I said innocently. I stood to help my mom clear the table. It was something I'd do anyway, but it also felt good to move around. I had no doubt that before the weekend was over, I'd be forced to have a meaningful conversation with my parents about Vee and Natalia and my mistake of a lifetime.

I hadn't told them much over the phone. It seemed like a conversation that would be easier to have in person. And also, I'd simply preferred to put it off as long as possible, and luckily my parents seemed okay with letting me get through at least the first few hours here without discussing it with any level of seriousness.

"Did Liam text you?" my mom asked as she wrapped up the leftovers. "I told Mrs. Walker you were coming down this weekend. She said she'd let Liam know. You haven't seen those guys in a while, have you?"

Mrs. Walker was Liam's mom, and Liam and I had been inseparable for most of our childhood, along with our other buddy, Crispy.

"Not really," I said.

Like most guys, we texted here and there or liked each other's posts, and from time to time got together when we were home for the holidays. But we didn't reconnect the way our moms would've liked us to, and that drove them crazy.

"You still talk to Crispy's mom too?"

"Of course. And I can't believe you guys still call him that," she said with an eye roll I could sense even though I wasn't facing her.

I still laughed whenever I thought about how he'd gotten the nickname.

"Crispy?" Vee asked as she got up to help with the dishes. My mom quickly shooed her away. There was no way she'd let a guest lift a finger. "I'm guessing there's a story behind that?"

"I'll let him explain when you meet him."

"So I get to meet some of your old friends?" Vee sounded excited, and for some reason, that surprised me.

"Sure. I'll text them in a little bit and see if they're free." I was beginning to get excited too. There was a good chance they'd be around. Liam had gotten a job in town right after high school, and Crispy had just moved back after he'd graduated in May. Now was as good a time as any for our trio to meet up, especially since it would be a welcome distraction from my current drama.

Adrien laughed. "I'm sure a dude named Crispy is always free."

Though there was probably some truth to Adrien's statement, I didn't want to let him know it.

"Why do you always have to be such a douchebag?" Nattie asked. "You're no catch yourself. You couldn't even leave the state to come here without asking your parole officer."

"I didn't have to *ask* him. I just had to *notify* him."

"Seriously?"

Grandma sounded almost impressed, but my dad leaned in close to Adrien. "Whaddya do? If it was anything havin' to do with an animal or a child, I'm gettin' back out the shotgun."

I watched as Adrien's normally tan complexion whitened. "No, not that. Um, I just..."

"He drunk drove a bike through the window of an ATM vestibule," Natalia was happy to explain.

I wondered if that was the real reason or if she'd made it up to avoid talking about any of their family's business dealings.

"See," my grandmother said to my dad. "That's why I never let you get a motorcycle. Can't control those things."

"Oh, sorry. I should've been clearer. It was a bicycle."

It made me think back to when Vee and I had left the bar and ridden my bike back to Minnie's to make the brownies.

My grandmother laughed loudly. "Hey, Roland, remember

when Bucky got that DUI riding Light Bulb?"

Light Bulb was the name of our neighbor Bucky's horse. Bucky was known to ride the animal to Smitty's, which was the only bar in town, when he didn't feel like walking the mile or so back and would be too inebriated to drive.

"Of course I remember." Grandpa let out a deep chuckle. "It's Bucky who doesn't remember."

"That poor horse," I said, thinking back to the incident.

"What happened?" Vee asked, sounding almost afraid to hear the answer she might receive.

"It's not *that* bad," I told her, not wanting her to think Light Bulb had been the victim of some sort of animal cruelty case or something. "Bucky used to ride the horse into town to the bar sometimes. They usually ambled along leisurely during the journey home, but one night during a horrible snowstorm, Bucky was in more of a rush to get home, so he encouraged Light Bulb to go faster. But because of the weather and the dark, neither of them could see well, and Light Bulb ended up crashing into a car that had gotten stuck in the snow."

"Oh my God," Vee said.

Natalia brought her hands up and steepled them in front of her mouth. "Was he okay?"

"Light Bulb was fine. The car was in worse shape than the horse, and there was no one inside. But during the impact, Bucky was thrown off into a snowbank. He must've gotten knocked out because he didn't wake up until the next morning."

My dad added, "Only reason the stupid bastard didn't freeze to death was because his horse slept near him and kept him warm enough all night. The Millers found them huddled together when they went to get their car the next morning."

"I didn't think it even snowed much down here," Vee said,

still laughing from the story.

"Doesn't," my grandfather said. "Lived in Virginia my whole life and I can count on one foot the number of times it's snowed anywhere close to that."

"Who counts on their feet?" I asked.

Grandpa raised an eyebrow like I was the strange one. "Seems harder to count on your hand, don't it?"

"But...shoes," I said.

"Enough with this hands and feet business," Grandma interjected as she stirred the tea my mom had set down a few moments ago. "You two are gonna make me get the shotgun out again."

God, had I missed my family.

Chapter Seventeen

VERONICA

I was pleasantly surprised by how smoothly lunch had gone. I didn't think I'd escape the weekend without having to fully face the situation that was my current life, but at least Owen's family had given us all some time to settle in without asking us to explain how the hell—or *why* the hell—any of this had happened.

His friends, on the other hand, weren't so forgiving.

They gave us all of about forty seconds before Liam asked, "So which one's the girlfriend, and which one's the wife?"

Liam reminded me a bit of Owen with his light, floppy hair and easy smile, but he stood a few inches shorter and wore dark-framed glasses, which added a level of seriousness and professionalism that Owen lacked.

"I'm the wife, but I guess you could say we have an open relationship," Nattie explained, her expression full of seduction and sweetness. Real fucking subtle. "And Veronica's the—"

"*Ex*-girlfriend, actually" I cut in, still not ready to put such a formal title on whatever Owen and I were. It felt too soon, too permanent, too . . . jinxed to attach any labels to it.

But the expression on Owen's face when I cast a glance in his direction told me he felt differently.

"Ooh, interesting," Liam said, pouring himself some more beer from the pitcher we'd ordered for the table.

"Why's that interesting?" Owen asked. "I wouldn't have gotten married if we were still together."

"Because you two didn't do anything wrong," Liam said, gesturing to Nattie and Owen. "Technically speaking. You know, if you weren't together."

I shrank inside a little at his words, but I did my best to appear unaffected. Because there it was—the crux of it all, the first domino to fall in a line of many. If I hadn't been so insecure, so unsure of Owen's ability to remain the man I knew him to be, maybe I'd be meeting his family and friends as his girlfriend and not playing third wheel to some fucked-up sham of a marriage everyone wished never happened.

Owen didn't reply, and I wondered if it was because he couldn't think of anything that would've been worth saying, or he didn't want to make the whole thing worse by saying the wrong thing.

"Can we talk about something else?" Nattie asked suddenly. "I think we've all relived this disaster enough for now."

I typically didn't support Nattie's suggestions, but this time was an exception.

"I agree," I said.

Nattie gave me a small smile, and for the first time, I realized that this wasn't only hard for me. It was hard for Owen and her too, even if they were somewhat to blame.

And maybe I felt that way because I was somewhat to blame too.

"So," Adrien said, "what do you do for fun in this town?"

"You're lookin' at it," Crispy said. "Not the most exciting place, but it's home, and I can't seem to find any other place I'd wanna call that."

Unlike Owen and Liam, Crispy had dark hair, dark skin, and a beard that he kept long but well-groomed. He hadn't spoken much since we'd gotten here, other than to introduce himself and make the occasional comment. For some reason, it surprised me that he seemed more reserved than Owen and Liam. With a name like Crispy, I figured he'd be full of crazy stories. Instead, he struck me as the type of guy who listened more than he spoke, which was why I hadn't asked him to explain his nickname.

"What'd you do before you were old enough to drink?" I asked.

Liam looked at his two buddies before saying, "We drank."

"Just not in a bar," Crispy added. "We were fans of the woods, abandoned houses, the school bleachers."

"Could've never gotten away with that shit in the Bronx," Adrien said. "There was always someone around, and our neighborhood was pretty tight-knit. Everyone knew everyone and their business."

Even though our family didn't always abide by the law, the last thing they wanted was for us kids to get in trouble with it. It would've brought more unnecessary attention onto my family.

"To be fair, our town is like that too," Crispy said, "but I guess there's a lot more open space around here. Makes it easier to fly under the radar."

"Oh yeah," Owen said with obvious sarcasm. "You're super stealthy."

We all turned our heads toward Crispy, who looked like he might be pretending to be offended. Rolling his eyes, he breathed deeply before opening his mouth. But instead of words coming as I'd predicted, he simply sighed. It was the kind of sigh that let you know there was something worth hearing if the person were willing to share it. But it didn't seem like Crispy was.

"What is it?" Adrien asked, looking more at Liam and Owen than at Crispy. Even he'd seemed to pick up on Crispy's reluctance. The story had to be a good one.

"Don't look at me," Liam said. "I wasn't even there for it."

"May as well tell 'em, because whatever they're imagining is probably worse than the truth," Owen said.

"You really didn't tell them the origin of Crispy?" he asked Owen, obviously skeptical.

"No, man. It's your story," Owen said.

Owen had put his phone in the center of the table with Crispy's and Liam's—a tradition they said they'd started a couple years ago when they got together so they wouldn't be distracted when they got together. Apparently the first one to pick his up had to pick up the tab too. And Owen's had already buzzed a few times.

"Why don't you get that?" Liam suggested, giving a nod toward the phone. "Could be important."

"Nope. All good."

Crispy began telling his story, and once he got going, I was surprised by how captivating he was since he originally seemed a little shy. But as he told us about how he and Owen had sneaked into someone's barn to get some cows one night, everyone listened with full attention—even Owen, who'd been there to witness it live.

"Wait, why were you getting cows?" Natalia asked. "Did I miss something?"

"I'm confused too," Adrien said.

And though confusion wasn't an uncommon state for both of them, this time I needed more of an explanation too. But I figured Crispy would get to that.

"We needed them for school," Crispy answered.

That seemed to confuse Adrien even more. "You all got some weird-ass homework in the South."

"We wanted to get the cows to put on the third floor of the school for a prank," Crispy said. "Cows will go up stairs, but they won't go down unless they're forced to. We were seniors and basically wanted a day off, so we figured if we caused enough chaos, however harmless, they'd have to shut down for the day. No way they'd let a bunch of cows wander around the top floor of the school, and it would be difficult to get them down and out of there with students and teachers around."

"So what happened?" I asked.

"Well," Crispy said, smiling. It looked like the beginning of a laugh more than a result of a fond memory. "Owen got two cows, and I got two, and somehow we got them over to the school and inside with no problem." Crispy leaned in like what he was about to say would be something none of us would want to miss.

"And then what?" I asked, leaning in toward him also like I was privy to a secret others might not be.

"And then . . ." He looked back and forth slowly at all of us. "We brought the cows upstairs like we planned. But we heard a noise coming from the cooking room. I sent Owen to check it out, and the scream that came from him was a sound that'll haunt my nightmares for the rest of my life."

All of us looked to Owen to continue, and he simply said, "The cooking teacher, Mrs. D'Martino, was holding a spatula." I thought he looked almost catatonic as he spoke. But Crispy, on the other hand, seemed to be holding back a laugh.

"Where was the spatula?" Crispy said quietly to Owen, the way a therapist might speak to a traumatized patient.

"It was in her . . ." He swallowed hard, and we all probably knew where this was heading. But Owen continued anyway. "In her asshole."

Nope. Not where I thought this was going.

"Holy fucking shit!" Adrien said. "Was she hot?"

Jesus Christ.

"So she was just . . . what?" Natalia asked, looking completely disgusted. "Fucking herself in the ass with a cooking utensil?"

"Yeah," Owen said, still looking as frightened as if it'd happened moments ago. I guess an image like that tended to stay with you. "And Ms. Watts was helping her. Music teachers are always the most fucked up."

"You know," Liam said to Owen, "I can't believe I haven't thought of this before, but if you hadn't caught her, one of us might've used that spatula in cooking the next day. You saved our lives."

"I don't know if I'd go that far," Owen said.

It was definitely hyperbole, but one that still seemed fitting for the situation.

Adrien practically yelled. "Finish the fucking story already!"

Owen's phone buzzed again, and I saw him look down at his Apple watch.

Liam caught him too because he pointed at him and

yelled, "That fucking counts! You lose, Parrish!"

I'd expected Owen to respond immediately and tell Liam that was bullshit, that the deal was who touches their phone, and a watch wasn't a phone and he'd found a loophole. Instead, Owen said nothing. He just scrolled a little on his watch before clearing his throat and urging Crispy to finish his story.

"You okay?" I asked Owen quietly as Crispy continued telling everyone about how the teachers had screamed, scaring the cows, who then knocked over furniture. It sounded like I was missing the best part of the story, but I couldn't focus my full attention on it with Owen clearly agitated.

"Yeah," he said just as quietly. "Fine."

But his shaking leg and his teeth pulling at his lip told me differently.

"Who texted?"

"Oh, just this annoying dude from class. He never goes and was asking me what classes I have in the fall because he always asks for my notes. I should tell him to fuck off, but I never do for some reason."

"Cause you're too nice a guy," I offered, knowing the story was bullshit but not wanting to pry any further. Whatever Owen was dealing with wasn't my business. At least not anymore.

OWEN

"So the cow turned on the stove and it set your hair on fire?" I heard Natalia ask. "I don't even get how that's possible."

"Oh, it's definitely possible," Liam said. "He came to school the next day with most of his hair and eyebrows missing."

"Were the cows still there?" Adrien asked.

Their conversation faded into the background as I thought about the phone calls I'd missed. I hadn't realized who they were from until I got the text that followed. And now Vee was worried too, which meant that I couldn't grab my phone because that would only increase her suspicion.

"I'm gonna go to the bathroom." I stood abruptly, interrupting Crispy as he explained how his homeroom teacher had been the one to give him the name after Crispy said he'd burned his hair off lighting a cigarette. Better not to reveal that he'd fallen onto the stove trying to corral a cow running around the cooking room.

The group stared at me for a moment before going back to their conversation.

I walked around to the other side of the table where Adrien was sitting and kneeled down next to him. "Hey, wanna come to the bathroom with me?"

He looked at me like I'd just pulled up to his bus stop in a white van and offered him candy.

"What the fuck?"

"It's not … Just come with me," I urged through gritted teeth. "I'll give you twenty bucks."

By the time I made it to the bathroom, Adrien had caught up to me.

"Okay, where's my twenty bucks? And also, why are you being such a weird motherfucker?"

"Because your uncle's calling and texting me, and I have no idea why."

"I have no idea why either," Adrien said. "Twenty bucks," he said again, putting his hand out.

I pulled out my wallet. "Well, can you ask him? Vee already thinks something's up. I don't wanna look at my phone because then she'll know for sure something's wrong." I counted out a five and fifteen ones and handed it to him.

"You rob a stripper on the way here or somethin'?"

"Can you just call or text Ricky and ask what's up? Or I can do it. Just give me your phone."

"I'm not giving you my phone. How do I know you're not a narc?" Adrien narrowed his dark eyes at me, causing his thick eyebrows to press together. He could definitely be intimidating when he wanted to be.

"Are you for real right now? Why would I be a narc?"

He crossed his arms and puffed out his chest enough to make himself look bigger. "The better question is, why *wouldn't* you be?"

"Adrien, Jesus…can you *not* do this right now? You actually think I'd mess up whatever I have going with Vee again to rat you out to the police?" I lowered my voice enough that the guy coming out of the restroom hopefully didn't hear me as he walked down the hallway to the main part of the bar.

Adrien looked me straight in the eyes for at least half a minute before he seemed to decide my argument had some merit to it.

"Fine. I'll call him. But I'm not getting involved in… whatever this is between you two."

I took the phone from Adrien and opened the phone app before I realized I had no idea what Ricky's number was. Obviously, I'd never bothered to remember it. I had no reason to. Until now, that was.

"Can you find his number?" I asked, handing the phone back to him. "I don't wanna go through your contacts."

Adrien cast a suspicious glance at me as he scrolled through his phone. This fucking guy. When he handed it back to me, I looked at the screen and asked, "Does he know he's in your phone as Uncle Dick?"

"What do *you* think?"

I laughed softly as I pressed the call button and waited for Ricky to answer. It took longer than I expected for him to pick up.

"Yeah," Ricky said sternly.

"Hi, Rick...um, Mr. Diaz. This is Owen Parrish. I saw you called me and wanted to call you back."

"Why are you on Adrien's phone? What's the matter with yours?"

"It's turned off," I answered, not expecting the question. "I mean, I had to turn it off because it seems like it has a virus or something. I should probably get it looked at, actually."

"Probably the websites you're going to."

"Yeah, maybe." It took me a few seconds to realize what he probably meant, and I regretted responding immediately rather than processing his meaning first. "I think I clicked on one of those sweepstakes things a while back," I said, hoping to change his line of thinking but knowing I probably didn't.

"Listen, Owen, I need you to do me a favor while you're down in Virginia."

"A favor?"

"Yeah. You're familiar with favors, aren't you? If you need a definition, you'll have to handle that on your own. I'm not fucking *Webster*."

"No. Yeah, I know what a favor is," I told him, feeling like an idiot for how I'd responded. "How can I help?"

"There's a guy right outside of Richmond who has something for me that I need you to pick up. Can you do that tomorrow morning? You'll have to get there early because the guy's gotta be at work by eight thirty. You can just meet him in the parking lot outside the construction site he's on."

"Um, yeah. I think I can do that. Does Vee know the guy?" I asked, wondering how I would know it was him.

There was silence on the other end for long enough that I wondered if I'd dropped the call, but when I pulled the phone away from my ear to look at the screen, I saw the call time still ticking.

"Ricky?" I said with clear hesitation.

"Vee stays out of this, you understand? She doesn't know you're going, and she, under no circumstances, is to go with you. Got it?"

Shit.

"Yeah, of course. She won't know anything about it." This whole thing already scared the hell out of me. If he didn't want Vee going, or even knowing I was going, and he obviously didn't want to ship it, I was as sure as I could be that whatever he wanted me to pick up was something that I didn't want to get caught with. "If it's easier, I can let Adrien take my truck, and he can pick it up for you."

"Well, that's probably easier for *you*. But Adrien doesn't owe me any favors. You do."

"Right, yeah, you're right. Whatever you need."

"Good," Ricky said sternly. "Because I may need you to do a few other things before you come back home."

Fuck.

"I'll send you the address when we hang up."

"Okay, thanks."

"Make sure you get your phone fixed or whatever because this probably won't be the last time we'll be speaking."

"Will do." I wanted so badly to know what I'd be picking up, but I had a feeling that knowledge wouldn't do much to make me feel any better about the situation. The opposite actually. Knowing what I was getting into would probably make me less likely to do it, and I was worried about the implications of that decision. I needed to be on Ricky's good side if I had any chance of getting out of this marriage anytime soon. If only Natalia were Ricky's daughter and not their sister's, maybe he'd be more motivated to get the marriage annulled.

I heard the line go dead, and I pulled the phone from my ear and handed it back to Adrien.

"What was that about?" he asked, putting it back into his pocket.

Leaning against the wall, I wondered how my life had gotten to this point. I was married to the love of my life's cousin and hanging out in a hall near the bathroom of a bar in my hometown wondering how the hell I was going to pull off whatever shady shit Ricky had asked of me.

And I couldn't tell Vee anything about it. Though . . . Ricky hadn't said I couldn't mention it to Adrien. All Ricky had said was that Adrien didn't owe him any favors. Which meant that if I hadn't owed him a favor, Ricky probably would've asked Adrien to run his errand.

"He wants me to pick something up from some dude at a construction site tomorrow outside of Richmond. Any idea what it could be?"

Adrien's brows scrunched in thought, and he leaned against the opposite wall so people could pass us. "Not really. I can't even think of anyone my uncle might know down here. I mean, he knows people all over, but no one comes to mind. And if I don't know who it is, it makes it tough to figure out *what* it is."

"You think it's drugs?" I asked.

I'd never messed with anything other than weed, and the thought of possessing anything more serious, let alone transporting them across state lines, scared the hell out of me. But I felt like that was the most logical explanation.

He shrugged. "Could be. But it could be anything, really. Weapons, dirty money. Oh," he said, sounding too excited for the conversation. "This one time he had me pick up something for him, and when I delivered it, he opened it up and there was a hand in there."

My stomach tensed with anxiety. "Like a human hand?"

"No, a fucking monkey's paw." He laughed suddenly. "You ever read that story? Some dude gets three wishes and somehow fucks everything up. It's the only thing I remember from any high school English class." He shook his head pensively. "Made me rethink a lot."

"What are you even talking about right now?"

"I just told you."

I tried not to overtly grit my teeth, but I was sure I was biting down so hard I might actually crack one of them. "Let's just go back to the table. I'm sure Vee's wondering what's going on."

"Man," Adrien said with a shake of his head. "She's got you on a short leash, and *she's* not even your wife."

This was gonna be a long fucking weekend.

Chapter Eighteen

OWEN

Once I got back to the group, I tried my best not to let myself get overly anxious about Ricky's request, but I was so preoccupied with my new mission I barely cared about Natalia hooking up a selfie stick she'd brought with her and taking a picture of all of us for the judge. At least she was trying to help.

I, on the other hand, was busy figuring out how to do something else that would probably end in complete disaster. Or possibly jail time. I didn't *know* it was something illegal. After all, why would he trust *me* with something that could land on him if I were caught? Or maybe he hoped that I knew better than to rat him out—which I did—and that if I were caught, I'd be the one in trouble and none of it would fall on the Diazes.

"So what's the plan for tomorrow?" Liam asked.

"The plan?" Why would he care about our plan?

"Yeah." I noticed him and Natalia exchange smiles. "Nat invited me horseback riding with you guys."

Nat? How long had I been in the bathroom hallway?

"Oh, we're doing that?" I knew we'd talked about it at

lunch, but I didn't think it would actually pan out for some reason, and now that I'd become a southern drug runner, I'd have to figure out how to balance the two.

"I'll go," Vee said. "I think it'll be fun."

"Probably," Crispy said. "Until one of you cowboys decides to race and Owen ends up face first in Wilma Nelson's garden."

Vee looked back and forth between Liam and me before she evidently decided the story sounded too specific to be made up.

"I feel you shouldn't be allowed near farm animals anymore," she said to me.

We both laughed before I said, "See, you're rethinking the chickens now, aren't you? Seriously though, Mrs. Nelson was pissed," I said, dragging out the word to emphasize how mad she really was. "She called my parents, and my mom made me replant her sunflowers because the ones I hadn't dug up completely with my fall had gotten squished."

"Ha!" Liam laughed loudly. "I totally forgot that."

"I didn't. She eyed me that whole summer every time I walked past her house because I never got her dumb flowers to grow back."

"Wait," Adrien said. "You were riding the horses in the street? That's dope."

"It was, in fact, dope," I agreed somewhat somberly. "There's a farm up the street from me that's owned by the family of another buddy of ours from high school. We used to take the horses out before we could drive. After the . . . incident with the flowers, Mrs. Nelson called the local driving school and tried to get the instructors to ban us from the class so we couldn't get our licenses. I guess she thought if we were that bad on horses, we probably shouldn't get behind the wheel of anything with an engine in it."

"We showed her!" Liam said.

Vee looked surprisingly interested. She leaned closer to me, resting her chin on her palm as she propped her elbow on the table.

"What happened?"

"They let us get into the next class for student drivers, even though technically there weren't any spots left for that session. They must've thought we really needed the course. Basically, it allowed us to get our licenses earlier than we would've if we had to wait to take the course."

"Is this Wilma Nelson person still alive?" Vee asked.

"Yeah, I think so," I said. "Why?"

A mischievous grin came across her face as she looked around at the rest of the group before letting her eyes settle on mine.

"Because we should totally ride some horses past her house tomorrow."

VERONICA

I woke up to Natalia knocking on the bedroom door and calling my name, but I rolled over to see the time before I decided to say anything back to her. It was only eight o'clock, which was essentially the middle of the night for her, so I couldn't even guess why she was already at my door, especially when we'd been out late last night with Owen's friends.

"Go away," I groaned, bringing the covers over my head again to block out what I could of her voice and the sun that was peeking through the edges of the blinds. At least it seemed like it was going to be a nice day.

"Open up. I need to talk to you."

I groaned loudly, but even if she heard it, I knew better than to think that my annoyance would deter her from bothering me. "What do you want? Why are you even up?"

"Because I need to talk to you," she said again.

"Come in, then."

The door swung open almost immediately, and Natalia plopped down on the bed next to me.

"Where's Owen?"

"He said last night that he was gonna go do some early-morning workout in some guy's garage."

"Ew. Who works out in a garage?"

I pulled the blankets from my head and stared at her. "Is this what you came in here to ask me?"

"No, obviously. I didn't even know he wasn't here until I came in."

"Then why *did* you come in?"

"Okay, so do you promise not to judge me?"

Now I was interested. Only slightly, but still interested.

"You know that's impossible for me," I joked.

But her question reminded me just how important my opinion had always meant to her. Neither of us had a sister, and with so many boys around, we'd only had each other to swap stories about friend drama, critique each other's outfits, and do each other's hair. The funny part was, she was older, though only by about a year. But still, she'd always sought out my approval like if whatever she said or did passed the Vee Test, other people might find it acceptable too.

Obviously annoyed with me, Natalia let out a groan. "I'm serious, Vee. This is serious."

She didn't look at me when she said it, and her lighthearted tone had shifted to one much more ... Well, I wasn't sure what, but it suddenly made me much more alert.

"What is it?" I was sitting up now, shifting myself in bed so that I could see her better. When she didn't answer right away, I touched her arm. "Okay, Nattie, now you're starting to worry me. You came in here because you wanted to tell me something, so tell me already. You'll probably feel better after you get whatever it is off your chest."

Nattie was quiet for a moment before she looked over at me. "I'm not telling you because it'll make me feel better. I'm telling you because I need your help."

"Okay," I said, my voice holding a caution I wished I'd thought to mask. Whatever this was, Nattie needed my support. She needed me to be stronger than I sounded at the moment. "Whatever you need."

Sure, I gave her shit. We gave each *other* shit. But when it came down to it, we were family. Not quite sisters, but the closest either of us had to one.

"I think I might be pregnant."

Chapter Nineteen

OWEN

"Hi, honeys, I'm home," I called as casually as I could. In truth, I was as happy as I'd been since last night, before I'd found out I'd have to take part in the transport of some sort of potentially illegal venture. Now that I was home and it seemed no one had followed me, I could breathe a momentary sigh of relief. Once I had to cross state lines in a few days during the five-plus-hour journey home, I'd probably need to take one of my grandma's Xanax to calm down.

The black box Ricky's associate had given me had been a little smaller than a shoebox. Not the most discreet item to hide, but I was happy it at least wasn't the size and shape of a casket. I'd easily been able to stash it in the garage behind some boxes when I'd gotten home since I didn't like the idea of driving around with it in my car if I didn't have to. I just had to remember to take the damn thing with us when we drove back. It was almost wishful thinking that I'd forget.

"Hello," I called again, hearing the house conspicuously quiet given the fact that in addition to my usually raucous family, we had three Diazes in the mix. Only Gimli seemed to hear me. He came running over, and I bent down to scratch behind his ears. "Where is everyone, bud, huh? Are they doing fun things without me?"

Gimli ran toward the back door and scratched at it. As soon as I opened it, he bolted out with an exuberance that told me he was off to get into trouble.

"Gim!" I called, chasing after him through the yard toward the small stream. He managed to jump the four feet or so across and dart all the way up the hill before I'd even gotten to the stream.

"Let 'im go," I heard my dad say from behind the shed. "He'll come back. You're not gonna catch him."

"Where is everyone?" I asked, looking around the side of the shed and over to the small barn.

"Dunno. I've been out here since six. Where'd you go drivin' off to so early? Figured you would've been in bed awhile longer with how late y'all were out last night."

"Oh, um, yeah. Figured I'd get an early start. Liam's apparently been on this health kick and wanted a workout buddy this morning." It was easier to lie to my dad when I didn't have to look him in the eye, so I was glad he was bending down to open a paint can and not looking at me.

"That's nice of ya." He looked up at me. "What'd you guys do?"

"What?"

"The workout. Run? Bench? Squat? What kind of exercises?"

"Kind of a mix of stuff."

I wasn't sure when my dad had taken an interest in exercise, or if he only cared because he cared about *me* and was trying to take interest in things I felt were important, but I needed to change the subject.

"You need a hand?" I pointed at the bucket.

"Nah, I'm all right. Coulda used your help a few weeks ago when I was sanding the old paint off this thing, though. What a pain in the ass that was."

I laughed and then grabbed the rolling pan and set it down in front of him.

"Thanks."

I looked around again. "You really don't know where anyone is?"

"They went to breakfast somewhere," he said with a smile. "Don't get too much time on my own here, so I'm gonna try'n enjoy it." He paused as if he was reconsidering. "Unless you wanna stay out here and talk about things."

"I will talk to you and Mom about all this. I know I need to. I'd rather do it when both of you are around, though." And also, I didn't want to discuss any of this while I was still raw from completing Ricky's errand.

My dad set the lid of the can on the grass nearby and turned toward me so he was fully facing me.

"Honestly," he said. "Mom was pretty hurt when she found out you got married. You know how she is. She wanted to dance with you at your wedding and get family pictures taken. But I told her she hasn't missed anything because there wasn't anything to miss."

"Nope. Just a night of drinking, heartbreak, and poor decision making," I told him.

Laughing, he said, "Think we've all had a few of those nights. You're just the only person I know who ended up married at the end of one of 'em."

That made me laugh too. It was so simple yet so true. My dad had never been one to mince words. He called it like he saw it and didn't tend to speak for the sake of adding words where they weren't needed. So when he talked, I tended to listen.

"I'll leave you to it, then," I said with a smile I hoped conveyed how thankful I was to have him in my life. "Let me know if you need anything."

"I won't," he said as he poured the paint into the pan.

And when I walked back to the house, I wondered if he'd meant he wouldn't need my help or wouldn't ask me for help if he needed it.

Then I realized it didn't matter compared to the rest of the shit I had going on in my life right now.

VERONICA

I asked Owen's mother if she'd be willing to drive us into town so we could pick up a few things at the drugstore that we'd forgotten to pack, and not surprisingly, she was happy to help. She even suggested that we get breakfast at a little diner nearby afterward.

I could tell Nattie was hesitant because she no doubt wanted to get back to the house and take the test, but even she knew it would be rude to decline the invitation. And once Jimi and Roland heard about the diner, there was no way they weren't coming along. They asked Owen's dad if he wanted to go out as well, but he said he had some outdoor projects he wanted to do this morning before it got too hot out.

Owen's family had seemed to forget about Adrien, which I was sure Nattie was thankful for, but as we were all piling into

Claudette's van, we heard, "Wait up."

Adrien was jogging down the driveway toward us. I should've known better than to think we could escape without him. He was a FOMO type of guy, so even though he probably didn't have any idea where we were going when he hopped in the van, he knew wherever it was would be better than staying in the house alone.

It turned out the restaurant was only a few doors away from the drugstore, so Claudette, Jimi, and Roland put our name in for a table, and we would meet them when we were done picking up what we needed.

"Whaddya forget?" Adrien asked once we all exited the car.

Natalia rolled her eyes, but I could tell she was trying to hide her anxiety by acting annoyed with him.

"Why do you care?"

"Just wondering how long you'll be. I'm hungry."

Claudette pointed toward the café called Jacqueline's to let me know they were heading over and would meet us there in a bit. I waved in acknowledgment and hoped Adrien would go with them.

"You're always hungry," I said. "Why don't you go with Owen's family? Maybe they have a muffin or something you can eat while you wait. That place seems like the kind of diner that bakes their own pastries."

His eyes narrowed at me like he was trying to see into my soul. Like the answer to whatever he was wondering was deep within me.

"It's weird to hang with his family on my own," he said after a moment. "And it sounds like you're trying to get rid of me, which makes me more interested in what you're doing here."

"Whatever," Natalia said. "Come if you want. You can help us decide which brand of tampons to get."

"Right." He laughed incredulously. "Like I'm gonna believe you both have your periods the exact same day."

"Haven't you heard of girls cycling together?" she asked.

It was a long shot but worth a try.

Adrien's eyes darted back and forth between us for a moment before he reached out for the metal door handle and pulled it open.

"After you," he said with a smile.

Any hope of being able to lose Adrien in the store was immediately dashed once I looked at the space. It couldn't have been more than twenty feet long, including the register and pharmacy. It had about six aisles total, consisting mainly of a first-aid section, different varieties of medicine, some baby items, and a family-planning section. We headed over to that while Adrien wandered over to look at the small selection of snacks they had near the register.

In an effort to get rid of Adrien, I prepared myself to talk loudly about the pros and cons of different absorbencies and ask Nattie if she'd ever tried a menstrual cup. Sure, it might make the few other shoppers uncomfortable, and it would be slightly embarrassing for me, but I was willing to do just about anything to get him out of here.

Luckily, he had the attention span of a preschooler on speed and quickly decided there wasn't much for him to look at in the small pharmacy.

"This place sucks," he announced loudly, earning a judgmental glare from the older gentleman stocking shelves who I assumed was the owner. "I'll just meet you at the restaurant."

He didn't wait for us to reply before heading out the door.

We both let out a sigh of relief. Natalia looked over the testing options, which weren't as many as I'm sure would've been available had we been at a larger store, but it was enough of a selection.

Natalia picked one up from the shelf and flipped it to the back. "This one does the little plus sign so you don't have to wonder about a faded line or whatever."

"How late are you?" I asked.

"I'm not sure exactly. Maybe a week or so." Her voice sounded oddly emotionless, and I wasn't sure if it was because she was reading the back of the box or because she was close to being in shock.

"Maybe we should get one of the early test ones so you're pretty sure about the result."

"Yeah, good idea. I knew you'd be good for something," she said, sounding more jovial than I was sure she was.

"Shut up," I said with a laugh. "I'm good for a lot of things."

After Nattie picked up the early test, we headed toward the register to pay. She threw a couple candy bars, a pack of gum, and some ChapStick on the counter. Then she placed a magazine full of recipes that we could've easily found online on top of all the items.

"What's with that stuff?" I asked with a nod toward the random shit she'd decided to grab.

"So no one notices the test."

"No one like who? I doubt anyone's gonna look in the bag when we get to breakfast. You can just put it in your purse."

The man we'd seen stocking the shelves eventually came over to ring us up.

"Find everything okay?" he asked.

Natalia nodded and said a quiet, "Yes, thank you."

He scanned the candy and the magazine and placed them into the bag. "Do you have a rewards account with us?"

"No," she answered.

"Would you like one? It'll only take a minute."

I smiled politely. "I think we're all set. We're only in town for another day or so."

"You sure? It'll probably save you some money today."

"Yeah, we'll pass, but thank you."

He scanned the pregnancy test, and Natalia glanced over at me uneasily as he brought the box closer to his face. He looked like a detective who'd just found a piece of evidence and was trying to figure out its importance in the case.

"You know, I think these are buy one, get one. If you want, I can walk back and look."

"We're good," Natalia said. "We only need the one."

"Suit yourself." He eyed both of us for a moment like he was trying to discern which of us the test was for before he set it into the bag. Once he was finished scanning, Natalia swiped her credit card, and I quickly grabbed the bag off the counter.

On the way out, I pulled out the test and shoved it into my purse. We walked past the shop next door, and as we prepared to enter Jacqueline's, I stopped right outside the door.

Turning to Natalia, I said, "I'm really hoping the father isn't that piece of shit Benny who didn't even bother to get you flowers for prom."

The way she looked down at the ground told me my attempt to lighten the mood fell flat.

"I hope there isn't a father at all," she said.

I wrapped my arms around her and pulled her in for a hug. "Me too," I said as I squeezed her tight.

Chapter Twenty

OWEN

While I waited for everyone to come home, I texted Ricky that I'd made it back to my parents' with the box. I hoped whatever was in it didn't need to be kept at a certain temperature since I'd stashed it in the garage. But since Ricky hadn't told me to keep it refrigerated, I figured I could at least cross off human remains from the list of things that could possibly be inside it.

"How was breakfast?" I asked once everyone had gotten back.

Vee leaned in to give me a kiss on the cheek. "Good. We missed you."

"Missed you too," I said, smiling inside and out. It felt good to be growing close to each other again.

"How was your workout?" Adrien asked.

"You'd know if you'd gotten up early enough to go." It wasn't true but seemed like an appropriate response.

"I don't exercise on vacation," he said. "Messes with my vibe."

I wasn't sure what his vibe was exactly, but I didn't want to ask either. Better just to change the subject.

"We still planning to go horseback riding in a little bit?" I asked, putting my arm around Vee and looking over at Adrien and Natalia.

Natalia looked at Vee, and Vee looked at Natalia as if both of them were waiting for the other to decide. They both seemed on board last night, but now they didn't seem so sure.

But now I needed something to get my mind off the fact that I was most definitely using my parents' garage to store Ricky's contraband. It was worse than when I hid a six-pack of beer in the walk-in freezer when I worked in a local pizza place in high school.

Every single one of them ended up exploding. Thankfully, my boss had agreed not to tell my parents as long as I forfeited my last paycheck after I was fired. Between the beer and the missed pay, that screw-up had cost me about a hundred and fifteen dollars. Whatever I'd put in the garage a little while ago could probably cost me a hell of a lot more than that.

"Hell yeah, we are," Adrien announced with enough excitement for all of us. "You got any cowboy boots I can borrow?"

"You don't need those to ride," I told him.

"Obviously. But if I'm gonna ride a horse, I wanna look good doing it."

"Ya can grab some of Roland's from our closet," my grandmother said to him.

"Thanks." Adrien had already made it to the stairs before he turned around and said, "You think they'll fit? Your husband's a pretty big guy. You know what size he is?"

"Not as big as they should be if you catch my drift."

I wasn't sure I did until she added, "Roland's a big man by

height and weight, but most of his extremities don't live up to the rest of 'im."

And with that, I understood fully. My grandmother had just indirectly commented on the size of my grandfather's penis. I wished I didn't have ears.

VERONICA

Owen had set up a time at a local farm where we could ride. Nattie, Adrien, and I would have to take some short lessons first, but after we got the hang of it, we could take the horses around the fourteen-acre grounds.

We arrived at the farm a little after two and were greeted by a middle-aged woman named Maura with long dirty-blond hair and a welcoming smile that emphasized the wrinkles around her eyes. She had a tan I imagined was probably year-round from spending so much time outside, and she seemed to love the horses like she would her own children.

"This one's name is Gracie," she said. "I think I'll have Adrien on her because she's a little bigger than the other two."

Adrien went over to Gracie and patted the horse on her side. Gracie moved her large brown head back toward Adrien and nudged him with it, causing him to jump back and yelp like a little girl who'd just seen a spider in her room.

Maura laughed a booming laugh that made me like her even more. "Gracie's blind in her left eye. She didn't see ya comin' up on her, and she startles easily sometimes."

"Oh." Adrien moved to the other side of Gracie and stroked her mane. "It's okay, girl. I'll take care of ya. You're gonna be my best girl, aren't ya?"

"More like your *only* girl," Natalia said, causing a few of us to laugh.

"I like this one," Maura said. "She's spunky."

Adrien shook his head. "That's one word for her. Not the one I'd use, but you haven't known her too long, so I get it."

Nattie glared at him. "Why did I bring you?"

"To Virginia or horseback riding?"

"Y'all are a cute couple," Maura told them.

The two of them looked so disgusted, they seemed to lack the words to correct her. At least Owen and I thought it was funny.

Maura showed me and Natalia to our horses next. Mine was a black female named Eleanor, who had a few patches of white on her side, and Natalia got a white one named Matilda, who Maura described as "feisty but sweet" like Natalia herself.

She got the first part right at least.

"You gonna take out your usual, Owen?" Maura asked.

"Of course. That dude's like a brother." Owen immediately began jogging over to one of the stables and was gone for a few minutes while Maura explained to the three of us how to get on and off the horse and some basic commands. By the time he emerged from the stable, riding a beautiful copper-colored horse, we were ready to ride too.

Though not as fast as Owen, who took his slow trot to a full gallop before stopping him on the edge of the fenced area that enclosed the rest of us. Maura explained that this was the training area, and not only would we need to get used to our horses, but they'd need to get used to us too.

We began riding slowly, and Owen's horse began trotting around as Owen led him, until the trot eventually changed into a full gallop. I never thought there would be a day when

I'd be impressed by how well someone could ride a horse, but apparently I'd been wrong, because watching how in control Owen appeared and how at ease he looked made me want to ride *him* later.

"Vee, Vee," I heard as a voice slowly became clearer, like I'd emerged from an underwater world that was all my own.

"Huh?" I turned toward the voice to see Maura on her own horse beside me.

"Did you hear what I said a minute ago? See if you can guide Eleanor over to that post where your friends are. Just give her a light tap on her side to get her going and pull back on the reins gently to slow 'er down."

I followed Maura's instructions and was surprisingly able to navigate us over to Adrien and Natalia. Owen came up to the other side of the fence with his horse, who he introduced as Brian.

"Do all the horses have human names?" I asked Maura.

"Sure do." She smiled widely and patted her own horse on the side of his neck. "These animals are better than people, if ya ask me. Most animals are."

I couldn't disagree with that. I loved Gimli, and I hadn't even known him that long. But the little guy was so full of unconditional love and affection, I couldn't imagine living anywhere without him now. I guess it was good I'd decided to stay at Owen's rather than move out.

"Kristoff was so wise," Owen mused.

"Huh?" Adrien asked, while Natalia and Maura stared at him curiously.

"The song from *Frozen*," he said.

When that didn't seem to clarify it for them, I added, "The kids' movie about the queen who can turn things to ice."

Still nothing.

"How have you never seen it?" I asked. Owen seemed just as shocked as I was.

Adrien and Natalia exchanged glances. "Um, because we're not five."

"It's a fantastic movie!" I said, somehow surprising even myself with my fondness for it. I wasn't usually one for children's movies, especially animated ones, but even I'd seen it.

"I'm not here to talk about movies," Adrien said. "I'm here to ride off into the sunset with Gracie." He patted the horse on the neck.

"Sun don't set for about six hours," Maura told him.

"Yeah. I . . . I know. It's just an expression." Adrien shook his head and let out what seemed to be a frustrated breath. "Can we just go?"

Maura looked at the three of us and evidently decided that the few minutes of training we'd had on our horses was enough.

"Guess nothing too bad can happen to ya out there." She turned toward Owen. "You still remember the trails?"

"Yes, ma'am," Owen said with a nod.

Maura opened the nearby gate, and the three of us managed to guide our horses out of the training area and alongside Owen.

"I'll start first since I know the way," he said. "The trails are pretty narrow, so we'll have to follow two by two."

"I call shotgun!" Adrien said excitedly.

Once Owen rode a little ahead of us, Adrien steered Gracie to her place next to Owen's horse, Brian. I'd expected Adrien to get thrown off immediately or for his horse to gallop away from him before he could even get on her, but somehow he'd seemed surprisingly adept at it.

I hoped Eleanor would behave just as well for me when I tried to get in line, and though we managed to follow, it didn't feel like Eleanor was as comfortable underneath me as I wanted her to be. Or maybe it was just that *I* wasn't as comfortable atop her as I would've liked.

Natalia seemed pretty uneasy as well. Matilda had random bursts of speed but then would slow to almost a complete stop when Nattie pulled back on her.

"What's going on?" I asked her. "Are you okay?"

"Not really." She tried tugging on the reins so Matilda would go toward Owen and Adrien, but the animal wasn't having it. "Why is my horse the only one who's drunk?"

"Just . . . don't be so . . . jerky. You're giving her anxiety."

"You two okay back there?" Owen called. He turned around as much as he could, but I doubted he could see us well from where he was at the entrance to the trees. "We'll wait for you here."

"Wait for us too!" I heard someone yell from the side of the field.

I looked over to see Liam and Crispy riding two nearly identical black-and-white horses. They must've come in from the street that ran along the side of the farm instead of the front entrance.

Since there was space between us and the boys ahead, Owen's friends took a place in line behind Adrien and Owen. After another couple of minutes, Natalia and I brought up the rear of the horse train, and Owen led us into the woods.

"I forgot Owen's friends were gonna come," Nattie said.

"You were the one who invited them."

"Yeah, but then...this morning came, and I was... preoccupied."

I knew she was talking about the pregnancy test, and even though Liam and Crispy were far enough ahead that they probably couldn't hear us, I guess she wanted to be certain no one overheard. Once I'd had time to think about it, I'd been wondering something that I hadn't really had time to ask her because there had always been someone nearby.

"So did you not think you might be...last night?"

She'd been drinking and hadn't seemed especially nervous or anything that would've made me wonder if anything was out of the ordinary.

"No. I should've because I'm never late. That bitch comes like clockwork every twenty-nine days. I just didn't realize what the date was until this morning, and then I panicked."

"Are you gonna take it when we get home?" She hadn't wanted to do it before we left.

"I guess so."

Liam moved a thin branch to the side as he rode, and it would've hit me right in the face if I hadn't been paying attention. At least our horses seemed to be following easily now that we were on a trail.

"Well, it's better to know, right?"

She didn't say anything.

"Oh my God, Nattie. It's better to know."

She looked over at me, and as she did, she pulled on Matilda's reins enough to make her think she should turn toward me. Nattie realized and corrected her quickly.

"Is it? Because right now it doesn't feel like that. It feels like I want some more time where I can pretend everything is normal and I don't have to figure out how I'm gonna tell my parents. You know them. Would you want to tell them something like that?"

The question was rhetorical, and I understood why. While my dad wouldn't be exceptionally pleased to hear his only daughter had gotten pregnant before I was ready by someone I knew wasn't ready to be a father, my dad would support me however he could.

I couldn't say the same about my aunt and uncle. They were kind people who would do almost anything for those they loved, but that offer didn't extend so far as to help raise their grandchild. I truthfully didn't know how they would react to that news should Nattie have to tell them that, but I knew it wouldn't be well-received. And for the first time in her life, my cousin might be forced to fend for herself if she was going to have the future she wanted and deserved.

The realization made me feel lonely in a way I didn't think I could ever understand. It reminded me of Minnie and June, and it broke my heart.

"No," I answered. "I wouldn't."

I watched Natalia bounce uncomfortably up and down on Matilda as the horse walked slowly along. Natalia stared straight ahead of her, but she seemed to be looking at nothing in particular. I wanted so badly to tell her that whatever happened, it would be okay. But that was a lie so cliché it had lost its meaning entirely. Because I knew as well as anyone that when life threw you shit you couldn't handle, nothing about it was okay.

So I told her the only truth I knew for certain. "Whatever happens, I'm here for you." I waited until she looked over at me, and her expression seemed a little more full of life. "We'll get through it together."

It was a moment that was so rare between us I felt like I needed to emphasize it with some sort of touch. So I reached my hand out beside me for Natalia to take it. And when she did, she leaned over so far she tipped completely off her horse.

Thank God for distractions.

OWEN

"So what'd y'all think?" my mom asked when we returned home.

I figured Vee and Natalia were both dying to take showers, and Adrien was walking like he still had the horse underneath him.

"It was really fun," Vee answered with a smile that looked genuine.

I wished I could've been closer to her on the trail, but I was glad she seemed to enjoy it.

Natalia muttered, "Yeah, we had a good time," but she didn't seem as enthusiastic as I thought she'd be, especially since she'd seemed so excited about it beforehand. "I think I'm gonna go take a shower," she said, already heading for the stairs.

"I'll go up with you," Vee told her.

Adrien watched them go up the stairs. "Shame that's my sister and cousin or it'd be pretty hot."

There were so many things wrong with that statement. Which really shouldn't have surprised me since there were so many things wrong with Adrien, but I chose to simply say, "I don't think they're taking a shower *together*."

"Never know. Maybe it's like when they go to the bathroom

in pairs." His eyes lit up. "What if all girls started showering in pairs?"

"Don't you have something you can go do? On your own," I clarified. "Away from here."

"Fine, fine." Adrien waddled into the kitchen and opened the freezer, muttering that he was going to go lie down and ice his balls.

When he came back to the living room with a bag of frozen peas, my mom said, "Make sure you throw those out when you're done."

Adrien seemed a little confused about why she'd choose to dispose of an unopened bag of vegetables, but he agreed without questioning her and then headed upstairs.

Once my mom and I were alone, she said, "How about some sweet tea?"

Sweet tea had always been my mom's way of suggesting we have a talk about something. When my parents wanted an explanation for why I was failing two of my classes during my freshman year of high school, she offered me tea before pulling out my report card and placing it on the table. When I moped around for two weeks during the summer before seventh grade, she made a pitcher and poured me glass after glass before I finally admitted that I was worried my crush Bethie Scott had seen my butt crack when I'd gone off the diving board.

My mom's sweet tea was like a nonalcoholic whiskey. It made me loose-lipped and somehow strangely emotional. And I knew this time would be no exception.

I also knew that—with the exception of violent crimes— no matter what I said or did, my parents would always have my back, even if they didn't particularly want to.

I watched my mom move around the kitchen, grabbing

the iced tea from the fridge and taking out three glasses from the cabinet. It meant my dad would be participating in this little intervention as well. It was preferable to talking to them individually.

Taking a seat at the kitchen table, I wondered what exactly my parents were going to say to me. The last time we'd had a discussion like this, I'd been living under their roof, and they were responsible for my actions. But this time none of what I'd done involved them. They didn't have to correct anything or answer to anyone about my behavior.

Though I did hope they'd *understand* it.

My mom called out to my dad, who had most likely been in and out all day doing work around the property. A minute or so later, I heard the screen door open, and my dad's heavy steps enter the screened porch. I saw him kick off his shoes before coming inside the main part of the house and heading to the sink to wash his hands.

After drying his hands with a dish towel, he turned around to face the table where my mom and I sat. "Shit, I didn't know this was gonna be"—he gestured toward the glasses and pitcher—"iced-tea serious. Claudette, the boy's a man now. He can make his own decisions because he's the one who's gonna have to live with them."

My mom waited until my dad took a seat across from her before responding. "I think our son getting married is something that affects the entire family, don't you?"

I watched silently as my dad's eyes darted back and forth between mine and my mom's. If he was looking to me for help, he might as well give up immediately. There wasn't anything I was going to say or do to make this any better. I just had to let my mom say her peace and hope she'd move on from there.

"She's got a point, son."

Shit. I should've known my dad would always take my mom's side. They'd been a united front ever since I was little, and I doubted that an impromptu marriage was going to be the situation to change that.

"Well, hopefully we won't be married for much longer. We'd already have it annulled if the judge would've allowed it. I think he wants us to learn our lesson. I wish I could tell him I'd absolutely never marry a virtual stranger again, but I don't think he'd believe either one of us or care."

My mom took a deep breath and looked directly at me before raising her hands so her palms were facing me like she wanted everyone to give her a moment to think. So we did.

"Can we just...backtrack a little please," she asked me calmly. "Like can you just tell me again how all this happened?"

"Does it really matter? It won't change anything," I said, knowing I owed them an explanation but not wanting to give one. I didn't say it sarcastically or with any sort of malice behind it. It was a simple statement of fact.

"Pretty sure when you're talking about somethin' like this, details are important. So why don't you humor us?" My dad had never been much of an analytical guy when it came to emotions, especially love. He was more of a *let's find a way to fix it* type of guy. To him, my marriage was just a problem that needed a solution, and since I had one in the works, I'd hoped I wouldn't have to rehash all of it, though I knew that was wishful thinking.

So I told them every detail about the night I could remember all the way up to the next morning when literally and metaphorically my mistake was brought to light and I had to face Vee's family.

My parents were quiet as I spoke, allowing me to share everything without any interruptions or questions. When I was done, my mom took a deep breath and hung her head.

She didn't have to say anything at all for me to know how much I'd disappointed her. It was in her body language—the way her shoulders fell and her eyes began to glisten.

She reached out to squeeze the hand I had resting on the table, but I beat her to it and grabbed hers first.

"I'm so sorry. I am."

"Sorry don't wet a fish," my dad said. It was a saying I'd become familiar with over the course of my childhood because I was no stranger to fucking up and then apologizing for it later. But like my dad explained the first time he'd used the saying, an apology wasn't any good once the fish was dead.

My dad poured himself some more iced tea. "So an annulment... that's like it never happened, right? Like when ya turn eighteen, any record you have gets wiped. Seems to me it's kinda the same thing."

I knew my mother wouldn't see it that way, but I appreciated him trying to soften things for her sake.

"Look." My mom put her hand over mine and squeezed it gently. "I know this isn't my business. Not really anyway. You're a grown man, and you make your own decisions. But as long as I'm still in this world breathin', you're my baby boy and I'm your mom." She said the words confidently, sternly even, but I knew my mom better than to think there was no sadness behind them. The pain I'd caused had extended far beyond Vee and myself. It made me even more afraid to face Vee's dad again.

Everyone remained quiet when my mom finished, and she forced a tight smile that seemed to signal it was okay for me to speak again.

Only I didn't know what to say. I knew better than to think any words could fix any of this for Vee or me or anyone else.

"I know I let you down," I managed to say. It was such an understatement it almost wasn't even worth acknowledging. "All I can do is promise that going forward, you'll be invited to all my future weddings."

That earned me something that resembled a genuine smile. Or at least the start of one.

"Why do you have to be such an ass?" she asked.

"It's probably genetic," I said, looking at my dad, who didn't bother to disagree. "Seriously, though. Vee and I have kind of decided to give our relationship a try again and just take things slowly to see where they lead."

"I doubt Mom would've taken my ass back if I married a relative of hers," my dad said. "You're a lucky guy."

I hadn't thought of it that way until now. I'd been so wrapped up in the problems that I didn't stop to appreciate some of the things the universe had helped steer my way. Vee could've never spoken to me again, but instead we still lived together and were trying to get our relationship back on track. And who knew ... Maybe when this was all behind us, we'd be stronger for it.

I had to hope so anyway.

Chapter Twenty-One

VERONICA

"My hands are shaking too much. You have to do it." Nattie looked up at me from the toilet.

"That's not really how pregnancy tests work," I told her.

She held out the stick toward me. "I don't mean you use it instead. I just need you to hold it because I feel like if I do it I'm gonna get pee all over it, and the directions said not to get any in that little window."

I was more concerned about getting it on my hand than the window, but I knew Natalia was having an internal—possibly soon to be external—meltdown. So I did the only thing a loyal cousin could do. I took the stick from her, put it between her legs, and prayed this would be quick and peeless. At least the shower was already running, so I could hop in if I needed to.

I shut my eyes, which admittedly wasn't the best idea, but it was a reflex I couldn't find it in myself to reverse.

"Okay, you ready?" Natalia asked.

"Just do it," I said before I changed my mind. Apparently the Nike slogan was appropriate for more than just athletics.

"Actually, you know what?" I stood up and grabbed a bathroom cup off the sink. "Pee in this. Then if you're shaking, it won't affect the test."

Natalia took the cup, somewhat reluctantly. It was small, and she was probably worried she'd pee on herself, but that beat peeing on me, so it was definitely the better option.

I turned around to give Natalia whatever sense of privacy she had left after having my hand near her vagina, and once she was done and both of us had washed our hands, we sat next to each other on the edge of the bathtub while we waited the two minutes.

Nattie picked at her fingernails as we both sat in silence. There wasn't anything left to say. I knew she was scared. I was scared *for* her.

After the timer on my phone counted down the last few seconds, I looked over to her. "You want me to look, or you want to do it?"

"I'll do it," she said after a moment. Then she took a big breath in and stood, looking somehow more composed than she'd seemed all day.

She picked up the test and studied it closely. "Oh my God," she said quietly.

"It's okay, Nattie."

"Oh my God," she said again. "It's negative. It's negative!" she said louder. "I haven't been this excited after a test since I passed my tenth grade English final and realized I didn't have to repeat the class!"

"I'm so happy for you." It sounded strange to say to someone that I was happy they weren't having a baby, but we both knew that she was even less ready to be a mother than she was ready to be a wife.

OWEN

We'd finished the day off by barbecuing some burgers and chicken in the yard. My grandfather took the opportunity to show off the motorcycle he'd fixed up but never rode. He was more than thrilled that someone—Adrien—finally cared enough to take interest in it.

Nattie and Vee spent most of the evening chatting with my mom and grandmother. Not surprisingly, they brought out the old photo albums of me and showed them pictures I didn't think I'd even seen before.

We planned to get an early start tomorrow to head home, so I packed up whatever I didn't need for tonight or tomorrow morning and put it in my truck so there was less to do in the morning.

Vee did the same, but Natalia and Adrien decided to wait until tomorrow. When I put our bags in the bed of the truck, I also got the box I'd picked up for Ricky and stashed it in a lock box that was attached to the side of the bed. At least by the end of the day tomorrow, I wouldn't have the thing anymore.

For a short weekend, it'd felt both long and exhausting. Apparently Vee must've felt the same because she was already dozing off when I got out of the shower and came into my bedroom around ten. Still clothed, she was curled up on top of the blankets without being under any of them. I grabbed an extra from the hall closet and carefully laid it on top of her, hoping not to disturb her.

At first I thought I'd succeeded, but as soon as I crawled into bed next to her, I heard her mumble, "When did we get so old?"

I assumed she meant it in reference to the relatively early time, though I hadn't really thought anything of it.

"We're not old," I said. "We're ahead of our time."

I heard a soft laugh, though it was muffled because her face was partially against the pillow.

"How do you always have a way of spinning things so they seem better than they are?"

She'd flipped over so she was looking at me, and I took the opportunity to brush her dark hair behind her ear and kiss her forehead. We hadn't had much alone time other than the previous night, but I'd been so preoccupied by the errand Ricky had assigned me that I hadn't even appreciated the chance to sleep in the same bed with her.

Now my body and mind were both acutely aware of how perfect this felt. She wiggled in closer to me, and I pulled her in tighter. She smelled like citrus and spearmint and... well, maybe still a little like the horses, but we probably all did, and that only made me love her even more. She'd fit in so effortlessly to the world I'd grown up in, and during such a stressful weekend.

"You know, you're pretty amazing," I said.

"Well, yeah. It's about time you noticed."

"I noticed when I first met you."

Smiling, she leaned in to kiss me, but it didn't last nearly as long as I would've liked for it to.

"You think your family liked me?"

I pulled back a bit, surprised at her question. "Of course. Why wouldn't they?"

"I don't know. I didn't really get a chance to talk to your parents privately or anything, so it's hard to tell, I guess."

"I think my mom knew you felt uncomfortable this

weekend . . . given the circumstances. I don't think she wanted to add to that by putting any more pressure on you." Giving her a kiss on the forehead, I said, "Maybe once I'm divorced, we can come back and visit as a real couple."

I tried to sound lighthearted when I said it, especially the part about being divorced, but the sentiment was real. I wanted Vee as deeply intertwined in my life as she was willing to be.

"A real couple," she repeated. I thought I saw her eyes sparkle as she said it. "Does that mean I get to wear your letter jacket and hang your picture in my locker?"

I nodded slowly. "Mm-hmm." I rolled her over onto her back quickly and positioned myself above her. "It also means we get to do this," I said before leaning down and kissing her like I'd been away at war for the last two years. Her mouth was warm and wet, and it brought back memories of when I had more than just my tongue inside it.

But this right here was so much more than sexual. It hadn't been easy to get back to this place, and we still had so much further to go. But I didn't want to think about any of that right now. I only wanted to be here in this place with Vee wiggling and moaning beneath me, begging me to go further, touch more of her.

I'd wanted this for so long—for Vee to want me like she did before I'd royally fucked up. Running a hand along her side, I brought her shirt up to pull it over her head. We took our time, exploring each other's bodies like we were discovering them for the first time. Every birthmark, every shiver—no matter how slight—felt new and exciting.

By the time both of us were fully undressed, we were practically writhing against each other.

"Please," Vee said, grabbing hold of me and positioning

me at her entrance and rubbing my tip over herself.

"What do you want?" I huffed. "Tell me."

"I want…" Grabbing hold of my ass, she clenched hard into the muscles with her nails. "Jesus, you know what I want, Owen."

I waited a moment, teasing us both, before I decided I couldn't wait any longer. And I didn't want to. She gasped when I pushed into her, but we both quickly settled into a rhythm—a slow, steady build that brought us higher and higher until we both shattered in each other's arms.

As we lay wrapped up in each other while our breathing returned to normal, it felt good to know that this time, we'd happily help put each other back together after we'd fallen apart.

Chapter Twenty-Two

VERONICA

The next morning we'd gotten Owen's truck packed up the rest of the way, and after a breakfast of fresh eggs and RJ's famous blueberry pancakes, we all climbed into the truck and prepared to head back home. I hadn't expected to feel like I did when we left. I'd gone into the weekend thinking I would want it to end but came out of it feeling disappointed—maybe even sad—that we didn't have more time there.

Owen's family had been so welcoming and loving. They'd treated all of us like we were family, and when she'd hugged me goodbye, Claudette had squeezed me tightly and made me promise I'd come back soon. It was a promise I was happy to make. And as I watched Owen's childhood home get smaller and smaller as we reversed out of the long gravel driveway, I hoped I'd be back sooner rather than later.

"You still saying no to the chickens?" I asked Owen. "Those eggs were pretty damn good."

Shaking his head, he laughed. "Even if I wanted to, I'm not sure the township would allow it. I think you need more land than Minnie's property has."

"It's your property now, bruh," Adrien said from behind Owen. "You can do whatever you want."

"I'm not saying I wouldn't do it because the place is Minnie's. I'm saying it because I'm the one who owns the house now, so I'm the one who will be fined if I'm not allowed to have them." Putting his hand on my thigh, he turned toward me for a few seconds before shifting his attention back to the road. "Maybe one day."

I wasn't sure what that meant exactly. Was he saying maybe one day he wouldn't care if he got fined because he'd have the money to pay it? Or maybe he was saying that one day down the road we'd live somewhere we could have them in a home that we bought together.

Or maybe he was appeasing me for the time being, so I didn't bring it up again.

"Are you just saying that like George says to Lennie?"

Owen let out a laugh through his nose, but he didn't get a chance to say anything before Adrien leaned forward.

"Who are George and Lennie? They those dudes we rode horses with?"

I stared at him. "No. They were Liam and Crispy. What's the matter with you?"

"So much," he said. I could feel Adrien looking back and forth at us between the front seats. "But who are they? Anyone I know?"

"No," I said, shaking my head. "Not anyone you know."

Adrien settled back into his seat, obviously still confused.

I knew Owen would get the reference to the classic book, but I'm pretty sure the longest thing Adrien had ever read was the recipe he used to make protein pancakes, so there was no way he'd ever read a John Steinbeck novel.

"Listen," Owen said, glancing back in the rearview mirror, "I really appreciate you coming. I think it made it less awkward for everyone having you there."

Since when did having Adrien around make anything *less* awkward?

"Thanks, man. I appreciate that. Happy to help however I can."

"Well, it didn't go unnoticed, and to return the favor, I'm happy to drive you back home after we drop off the girls so you don't have to take the bus."

What has gotten into Owen?

We had a long drive back to Pennsylvania, and he'd just volunteered to take my annoying cousin another few hours and then drive back home again. How was I just now learning that Owen was a severe masochist?

"For real?"

He must have recognized the complete and utter shock in my voice because his head whipped toward me like my comment had startled him.

"Yeah," he answered casually like he'd just offered to pay for Adrien's cup of coffee or something. "It's not a big deal."

Owen turned back to focus on the road, but my eyes remained fixed on the side of his face. There was some short stubble over his jaw, which I loved the look of. I reached over to massage the back of his neck.

"That's . . . sweet."

I didn't realize that I'd had an expectation of his reply until he spoke again.

"Like I said, it's not a big deal."

He didn't turn toward me or connect with me physically in any sort of way. He seemed almost . . . dismissive of the compliment, but I wasn't sure why. Owen was definitely humble, but this seemed different somehow. Almost like he was embarrassed I'd pointed out how nice the gesture had been.

How had I gotten so lucky to have a man like this one? And why had I been stupid enough to throw it all away?

OWEN

The two-hour-or-so drive with only Adrien turned out not to be so bad. Maybe I'd just built up a tolerance to the guy over the past few days, but I was almost starting to enjoy his company. Almost. Vee would probably kill him if she ever found out he'd told me some of the stories from their childhood, but since I'd promised him I wouldn't, he'd live to see another day.

"I know you only drove me up here because you have to meet Ricky, but I still appreciate the ride. On the bus ride down to you, the dude next to me lectured me about hygiene and told me the best way to keep clean was to clean yourself with your own saliva."

"Like a cat?" I asked as I pulled up to the house where Adrien lived with his parents.

"Exactly like a cat," he said before hopping out of the passenger seat of my truck and shutting the door. He grabbed his bag from the back and came around to my window. "Thanks a lot, man. I actually had fun. You're a pretty cool dude." He reached through the window to shake my hand. "I approve of you being a Diaz."

"Um, thanks," I said, not wanting to point out that technically I wasn't a Diaz because men didn't usually take the woman's last name. Though the more I thought about it, the more that felt like an antiquated tradition that did nothing but perpetuate centuries' worth of female repression. "Are you talkin' about Natalia or Vee?" It didn't matter what Adrien thought, but I found myself asking the question anyway.

He placed both hands on my door and seemed to think hard about my question. "You know what... either. You choose, dude. The world is your oyster."

I wasn't sure the saying applied specifically to my current situation, but I appreciated the Adrien-style welcome.

"Thanks."

Adrien gave me a stern nod and tapped two times on my truck like he was giving permission for a cab to leave.

"Take it easy," he said. "And good luck with Uncle Ricky. Don't let him intimidate you. He's like a big teddy bear."

More like a polar bear who would rip my throat out if I crossed him, but I wasn't going to argue semantics with someone who was still learning proper English.

"Good to know."

And with that, Adrien left me to meet with the teddy/polar bear who'd be deciding my marital fate.

How was this my life?

X_0 X_0 X_0

"You got the shit?" Ricky asked when I pulled into the parking lot I'd agreed to meet him in. I felt like I was auditioning for a part in some sort of gangster movie, and I was pretty sure I had no chance of landing the part.

I hopped out of my truck and retrieved the *shit*, as Ricky had called it from where I'd kept it safe in the bed.

Ricky's eyebrows raised when he saw it like he was

surprised I'd managed to complete the task. Can't say I blamed him. Taking the box from me, he studied it closely, moving it so he could see all sides fully and then the bottom.

"You didn't let this get above eighty-five degrees, did you?"

What?

He hadn't said anything about that, and neither had the guy I'd met. Had they? Now I wasn't so sure. I figured my best bet was to redirect.

"Can you tell me what's in the box now?"

I don't know what made me ask something I didn't logically want to know the answer to, but for some reason, I found myself asking the question anyway. Maybe subconsciously I wanted to know my maximum prison sentence. Or maybe I just thrived on stress and piss-poor decisions.

Ricky cast an uncertain glance my way before taking out a knife to cut the tape from the box's edges. Then he set the box on the trunk of his black BMW and lifted the lid carefully.

"Hmm," he said as he stared into the box.

Whether it was a good *Hmm* or a bad *Hmm*, I wasn't sure, but it was probably the latter.

"Everything okay?" I asked after an uncomfortably long time in silence.

"Depends." He looked away from the box and over to me. "How do you feel about melted truffles?"

"A-About what?" *Did he just say truffles?*

After he reached carefully into the box and pulled out a brown blob that had probably once been a perfectly formed chocolate delicacy, I had my answer. He pulled off the wax wrapper from the bottom and brought it to his mouth slowly. Before taking a bite, he studied it once more, like even a small bite might cause his untimely demise.

"Doesn't taste quite as good as I remembered."

After a few moments of chewing slowly as he stared at me, Ricky crumpled up the wax wrapper and tossed it to the side. If this were anyone else, I probably would've gone and picked up the thing. Instead I opened and closed my mouth multiple times without allowing any sound to come out. I imagined I looked like some sort of robot that hadn't been programmed correctly.

Ricky's eyes opened wide, and he mimicked my jaw movements.

"You had me pick up chocolate?" I asked quietly.

A laugh escaped through his nose as he rolled his eyes. "Not just chocolate," he said. "Diane Mooney's raspberry truffles."

"Truffles," I repeated, still in disbelief. "I thought I was transporting body parts or something." I couldn't stop my voice from getting louder.

"Careful," Ricky warned. "Remember who you're talking to."

My hands went to my head and instinctively pulled at the ends of my hair. I let out some sort of strange groan that sounded like a wild animal in pain and then locked eyes with Ricky.

I tried to compose myself before I spoke. "Who I'm talking to? I don't even know who I'm talking to. I thought you were gonna help me and Natalia get an annulment, but then you send me on some crazy-ass mission and make me think I might get offed in the process. But I did it because I'll do anything to get my life back—to get Vee back."

I sounded frantic, a little unhinged maybe. But Ricky had made me both those things, so it was time he dealt with the repercussions.

"This," I said, pointing at the box, "isn't me. I don't pick up unknown shit for people and cross state lines with it."

"Except you did both those things," Ricky replied calmly. He brushed his hands together before reaching in for another piece of chocolate. "Truffle?"

"Jesus Christ," I said. I didn't care if I sounded frustrated, or angry even. "I thought I was transporting drugs. Or human remains."

"Well, if you thought you were bringing me human remains and you didn't think to keep them in some sort of temperature-controlled environment, you still have a lot to learn."

"That's just it," I said. "I don't wanna *learn* any of this. You had me thinking I was gonna go to jail—"

"I wouldn't've let that happen."

"No? How do I know that? I barely know you, and what I do know doesn't make me wanna put my trust in you." I stared at Ricky hard, willing him to see the situation through my eyes. He had to understand me. How could he not? But then that only meant that he didn't care.

Ricky stared back at me, and I expected his expression to grow angrier with every word, but instead his face remained blank, almost as if he was incapable of feeling any emotion at all. And that was a hell of a lot scarier. It was the cold expression of a serial killer. Someone who'd feed you pieces of your own brain with some spaghetti and tell you it was meatballs.

"You done?" he finally said.

I swallowed hard and wondered if my life would end in this parking lot. Maybe I'd be memorialized with a chalk outline right here in this parking space next to my truck. People would bring flowers and handmade cards. Photos of me would be tacked to the nearby wall so people would remember how full of life I was until . . . well, I wasn't.

Or maybe Ricky would dump me in the Hudson with cinder blocks chained to my limbs so no one would ever know what came of me.

"If you're gonna kill me, can you at least do it here so my family has closure?"

Ricky's brows pressed closer together. "What?" He seemed genuinely confused. "I'm not gonna kill you."

"You're not?"

"No. I'm not risking jail time on someone who isn't even a threat to me."

I stood a little taller and straightened my shirt. "Oh. That's good, then." Not the part about not being a threat because that part made me feel like a pussy, but being a pussy was better than being dead, so I'd take it.

"You're like . . . an ant or something. But not like a fire ant or any of the kinds that bite you. You're not even the kind that takes your food at a picnic or something. You're more like those teensy tiny ones that show up in your kitchen and wander around."

"Oh."

"You know the kind I'm talkin' about, right? They're just kind of . . . there."

"Yeah, I get it," I told him.

He seemed so lost in his ant analogy that he hadn't noticed I'd spoken.

"Like they don't *do* anything necessarily, but they're still annoying as fuck."

"Mm-hmm," I said quietly.

"Anyway, this errand was just a test to see if you could

handle the pressure, and as much as you say you can't, it appears that the opposite is true. So," he said, clapping his hands together hard, "I need you to do one other thing for me—"

"I can't."

"Oh, but you definitely can. And I told you I wouldn't let you go to jail, so there's nothin' to worry about."

I wasn't so sure.

"Plus, if you don't do it," he said with a casual shrug, "then I won't have the judge grant you that annulment, and then Vee'll get all angry again, and no one wants that. Right?" He smiled like he already knew what my answer was going to be.

I guess I did too. Because nothing about Ricky's new favor had been posed as a question I could say no to.

Chapter Twenty-Three

VERONICA

To say I had been surprised when I'd randomly heard from June was an understatement. While my thoughts strayed to her often, I hadn't expected to ever actually speak to her again. So when she called and asked me to meet her, I leaped at the chance.

June and I set up to meet at a small café she said was closer to her house than the bakery. The fact she didn't want to meet there made me sure she wanted to talk freely about Minnie.

Owen thankfully had to work, so I didn't have to lie about where I was going—if one didn't consider the fact I hadn't told him about June's call in the first place. I still wasn't sure why I didn't want to tell him. Looking into Minnie's past had been to set his mind at ease, but somewhere along the way, June's story had come to feel like something only I was privy to.

Even though I'd told him about her voicemail a while ago, he still hadn't asked to listen to it. Maybe I was doing him a favor by not sharing this meeting with him. Maybe he was ready to put all we'd discovered behind him. Maybe I was deluding myself in an effort to feel better about this whole thing.

So many possibilities.

But it was what it was. June had called me and had requested only me to join her—though she might have assumed I'd bring Owen, a possibility I was going to ignore for the time being—so I'd done what she'd asked. Besides, it might be easier to speak woman to woman.

There was clearly no end to how thoroughly I could convince myself of something when it suited me.

I walked into the café about ten minutes early, but June was already there, sipping on something in a mug. A half-eaten Danish sat on a plate in front of her. She must've been here for a bit already.

She was facing the door, so she saw me walk in. I smiled and gestured toward the counter to let her know I was going to grab something for myself before joining her.

Nodding once in acknowledgment, she went back to her drink.

After ordering, the barista said someone would bring my order over to me, so I joined June.

"It's good to see you again," I started. "How have you been?"

June smiled. "Probably as good as an old woman can be. How about you? Where's your young man today?"

Shit. So she had expected me to bring Owen. "I've been doing well. We both have." *Other than the heartbreak we'd caused each other and the exhausting rebuilding of our relationship.* "Owen had to work today."

June broke off a piece of her Danish and chewed it thoughtfully. "It's so hard to get a good Danish these days," she said with a sigh, pushing her plate away a little so she could rest her arms on the table.

I took in the lightly tanned but thin skin covering her arms. Her fingers were gnarled, likely from years of rolling out dough. Moving my gaze up, I tried to see the resemblance in this elderly woman with the woman from the pictures. There'd been a joy radiating from the pictures as June and Minnie had stood side by side—a happiness that didn't stop at the smiles, but also emanated from the eyes as well.

Though the June sitting in front of me still took care of herself—it was evident in the way her hair was swept back in a barrette and the light dusting of makeup that hid some of her age—there was also a weariness to her. Something that ran deeper than a simple need for a nap. Something that had settled into her bones and stayed there.

"You're probably wondering why I asked you here," she said, her voice kind.

I smiled. "I'd be lying to say I hadn't been running through possibilities since you called."

She laughed and reached out and patted my hand. "I like you. I bet you keep your Owen on his toes." She retracted her hand, settling it on the table again. "I want to preface this by saying I am fully aware that neither you nor Minnie owe me anything. I'm already expecting you to say no, so don't worry about my feelings if you choose to do so."

That piqued my curiosity even more. What the hell could she want?

"When we were still . . . an item, Minnie gave me a locket. It had her and Milton's pictures in it. I treasured it. Never took it off. Until I did."

I stayed silent, intently observing June as she seemed to

grapple with the emotions surrounding this locket.

She took a shuddering breath, her gaze dropping to the table for a moment as she collected herself. When she looked back up, she had regained her composure.

"I gave it back to her when she left. When we *asked* her to leave. It was a cruel thing to do. It was bad enough we'd asked her to leave the house, but returning that necklace..."

June shook her head. "We'd already broken her heart, but when she'd taken that locket back from me, the light that had always been in her eyes went out. Like I'd...destroyed something in her." She let out a quick, harsh breath. "Maybe I was just seeing things and she was just walling herself off from us. I hope that was the case."

June fell silent then, seemingly lost in what I was sure were painful memories. I reached out and rested my hand on her arm, dipping my head down so I could make eye contact with her.

"How can I help?"

She gave me a watery smile. "I know I don't deserve it back, but...I'm not going to live forever. And when I go, I'd like to go wearing that locket. Maybe it's silly. She probably threw it away or pawned it. Even if you find it, she probably got rid of the pictures inside of it years ago. But whatever's waiting for us after this life, I'd like to have a piece of both of my loves with me." She laughed softly, but there was no humor in it. Only sadness. "I know it's selfish. I have no right to ask for something I so callously returned long ago. Like I said, I understand if you don't want to help me."

I sat back in my chair and observed the weary woman in front of me. She'd said she didn't deserve the locket, but... who got to say what we did and didn't deserve? She'd given up the locket, but she'd never given up her love for Minnie. And while it was shitty that she'd never let Minnie know any of that and shitty that Minnie had had to endure her life alone while June and Milton had seemingly moved on without missing a step, the truth was so much more complicated.

Not for the first time, I wished I'd known Minnie. Wished I'd known what kind of woman she'd been so I'd maybe have an inkling of what she'd want me to do.

But I didn't. I didn't know anything except what felt right to me in this moment. Heartbreak was a bitch—I knew it firsthand. Not the kind of bone-deep loss like June, Minnie, and Milton had experienced, but still, I felt I knew enough.

I also knew that the Minnie, who'd left her house and all its belongings to a college kid because she'd somehow decided he'd deserved it, was the kind of woman who took a chance. Who'd found it within herself to love again, even if that love had been maternal instead of romantic.

If I could fix even a fraction of what had been shattered all those years ago, then I had to do it, just as I had to fix what was between Owen and me. Love deserved a chance.

"We haven't found anything like what you're describing. I went through a lot of things Minnie had because we'd needed to sell some of it to finance the renovations to the house."

June's face fell.

"But there are a lot of places I haven't looked. Things I didn't sort through because they seemed more personal to Minnie. I can't promise you I'll find it. But I can promise that I'll try."

June smiled again. "That's all I can ask. More even than I should be asking. Thank you. So much."

"I'm happy to help," I replied. And I was. I just hoped Owen felt that way too.

OWEN

I came home from work to a quiet house, other than Gimli's nails clacking against the floor as he ran toward me.

"Hey, buddy," I said as I reached down to pet him. "Where is everyone?"

A thump from upstairs answered for him. It was muted, as if it hadn't come from directly above, but maybe the floor above that.

The attic.

As far as I knew, no one had been up there since we'd found the paintings. At least I hadn't.

"Should we go investigate?" I asked Gimli, who stared up at me with a doggy smile that let me know he'd follow me anywhere. Such a good boy.

I made my way up the stairs, Gimli on my heels, and into my bedroom. Heading for the closet where the access to the attic was, I noticed the light already on. So someone was obviously up there. I logically knew it was likely Vee since I doubted Nattie would have been able to find the attic, but a shiver worked down my spine anyway. What if it was an intruder? Or a poltergeist? The one that haunted my room had never seemed interested in following me, but things could have changed.

I took a deep breath and climbed the ladder. Once in the attic, I had a momentary second of panic when I didn't see anyone. However, upon closer inspection, I saw the top of a brown head peeking out from behind an open trunk.

"What ya doin'?" I asked Vee.

She jumped so severely, she flung forward into the chest,

causing the top to come down on top of her.

"Ow."

"Shit, sorry." I rushed to help, lifting the lid as she sat back, rubbing her head. "You okay?"

"Yeah. I didn't hear you come up."

"I was quiet in case you were a robber or something."

She smirked at me. "What would you have done if I had been a robber?"

"Sneak back downstairs and call the police from my truck."

She laughed. "Good answer." Vee held out a hand to me, and I grabbed it, helping her to her feet.

"What are you doing up here?" I asked.

Her eyes dropped to the trunk and then scanned the surrounding area that she'd clearly been rummaging through. "Oh, uh, just looking to see if there was anything else up here we could make some money on." She smiled. "I felt like a treasure hunter when I was searching for things before."

"Well, far be it from me to keep you from your pirate fantasies. Find anything good?"

"No, not really. What time is it?" Vee asked as she pulled her phone out of her pocket. "Oh, wow, I really lost track of time. Wanna get dinner?"

"Sure. Just let me grab a shower. Is Nattie home?" I asked as I made my way toward the steps.

"No, she said she was going out with people from work and not to wait up. Like I'm her mother or something. She's older than I am," Vee said with a scoff.

"Okay. Feel like anything in particular?" I made it back into my closet and waited for Vee to descend.

When she did, she seemed to be thinking. "Wanna just go

downtown and walk around until we find something that looks good?"

"Sure."

As I walked out of the closet, I turned to find Vee looking back up at the attic, biting her lip.

"Did you forget something up there?" I asked.

She startled slightly and then looked at me, a smile on her face once again. "No. Just got lost in thought for a second there."

"Anything wrong?"

She stepped forward and wrapped her arms around me, pressing her face to my neck.

"Nope. Everything's perfect."

And in that moment, it certainly was.

Chapter Twenty-Four

VERONICA

I was a terrible person.

Owen and I went out and had a wonderful dinner. Conversation flowed as readily between us as it always did, and there had been numerous opportunities for me to tell him about my meeting with June and why I was in the attic. But I didn't. Every time I opened my mouth to come clean, something held me back.

When Owen and I got home, we went up to his room to watch a movie. We cuddled, kissed, and allowed our hands to wander, though both of us kept it from turning into anything more.

"Earth to Vee."

I startled at Inez's voice in my ear. Looking around, I saw she and the other counselors were buzzing around, helping the kids clean up after lunch.

"Sorry."

"You doing okay?" she asked.

Inez and I had become close in the way work friends

did. We didn't hang out outside of Safe Haven but spent a lot of our work days together talking about random things and supporting each other through the rough days.

"Yeah, just got a lot on my mind. Nothing major," I replied as I got with the program and sprayed the now-empty tables so I could wipe them down.

She gave me a look that said she didn't believe me in the least.

I caved almost immediately, my shoulders drooping. "I'll tell you all about it once we get the kids outside."

She nodded in agreement, seeming very satisfied with herself that she'd gotten me to cave so easily. And ultimately, I *wanted* to talk to someone. And Inez was a good option since we didn't usually hang out in the same circles. And she typically gave great advice.

After the kids put their lunch boxes away and lined up, we headed outside. Roddie got a flag football game going while Inez and I oversaw a kickball game. Once teams had been made and play got underway, Inez and I settled back under a tree to watch.

"Okay, lay it on me," she said.

"It really isn't a big deal," I started.

"All the sighing you were doing tells a different story."

"I wasn't sighing."

She shot me a disbelieving look.

"Was I?"

"So much sighing. It was like seeing teen angst personified."

I laughed. "Are you calling me immature?"

"Never. Now spill."

I sighed, and she gave me an amused look, which prompted

me to glare at her. "Remember I told you about the woman named June who had been in the poly relationship with the woman who left Owen the house?"

"How could I forget? I am so here for that whole saga. Please tell me there's more."

"June called and asked me to meet last week." I shared the whole story with her about the locket and my agreeing to look for it.

Inez gave me a sympathetic look. "No luck finding it?"

"No. But that's not what's bothering me. Or at least not the main thing bothering me. Obviously, I want to find the locket for June. But I also realize a lot of that's out of my control. Minnie could've thrown it away for all I know."

"So what's bothering you that *is* in your control?"

"I haven't told Owen about the locket. I didn't even tell him about meeting with June."

Inez tilted her head slightly. "Why not?"

"I don't know."

She smirked at me. "Do you really not know, or do you just not want to say?"

"Both?" At her unimpressed look, I continued. "I don't really know why keeping it to myself feels so important. I've thought about it, and I think part of it's that he was close to Minnie, so I've kind of glommed on to June. But I also think it's maybe more selfish than that."

"How is it selfish?"

"Owen had this relationship with Minnie that was so special—she left him a house. And I guess I . . . want that. I want to be important to June the way he was to Minnie. Which is stupid because it's not a competition of who can be a bigger do-gooder. But I can't help it. I want to be the one to help June solve her problem. And I don't want to share the glory of it." I winced. "God, I really sound like an asshole."

Inez shook her head. "You're not an asshole."

"Well, I'm certainly something, and it's not a good something."

She laughed. "You're so dramatic."

I grabbed her arm and shook it. "Help me. Psychoanalyze me so I can fix whatever my problem is."

"That's going to be tough."

My heart sank. "Because I'm such a mess?"

"No, because there's nothing wrong with you."

I shot her an incredulous look. "There's definitely something wrong with me."

She smirked. "That's true. But not in relation to this."

"Funny."

That made her laugh. When she sobered, she shifted so she was facing me fully. "There's nothing wrong with having parts of your life that don't involve Owen."

"But I only know about June because of Owen," I argued.

"So what? You only have this job because you know Ransom. Do you call him up and tell him what you do here all day?"

"That's not even close to the same thing."

"It's only different because you've convinced yourself it is. Look, I get where you'd feel conflicted. But I'm assuming you plan on telling him eventually, right?"

"Yes," I said emphatically because I would tell him. Eventually. "I'd never give the locket to June without his say-so. Minnie left her things to him, and taking it would feel like stealing. But I don't want his help finding it, and I don't want to feel like I have to justify why I'm even looking. Not that I think

Owen would disapprove, but I don't even want to chance it."

"Because you have no intention of stopping?"

"Pretty much. Once I find the locket, at least we'll be discussing something that matters. Until then, we'd be arguing the hypothetical benefits and drawbacks of returning it. If it's a moot point, I don't even want to bother."

"Sounds logical to me."

"Even if a bigger part of me wants to be the hero and find it on my own?" I asked.

"Yup, even then. None of us are perfect, Vee. We don't get a lot of opportunities to save the day. It's okay to want to be the hero of the story from time to time."

I let that sink in for a moment.

"You're good at this," I finally said.

"Telling people how to live their lives? It's a gift."

I laughed. "I was going to say giving advice, but you're good at that too."

She smiled back. "If only I could get my own life in order, I'd be unstoppable."

My brow furrowed. "What's going on in your life?"

She groaned. "My landlord is being a douche. Raising rent every few months, but he won't fix anything. I should look for other options, but it's convenient, and even with the increases, it's still cheaper than anything else I can find that's even halfway inhabitable."

"That sucks. My friends know a lot of people in the area. I'll ask them to keep their eyes open for a decent place that's reasonable."

"Thanks." She let out a small gust of breath. "It's maybe just time to grow up and find a big girl job in some soul-sucking office somewhere or something."

I laughed. "Hopefully there are other options than that."
She didn't look convinced.

OWEN

Being Ricky's new errand boy was going to give me an ulcer.

It had never been more apparent that I wasn't cut out for a life of crime than when I'd had to give myself a pep talk to walk into a pool hall. It was the middle of the afternoon. How much crime could happen before dusk?

But maybe that was just a movie thing—that all seedy activity occurred at night. Maybe criminals realized they were underutilizing daytime hours and made the shift. What the hell did I know? Other than Ricky had called for me to pick up something for him at an address that led me to Rack 'Em Pool Hall.

I thought the name needed a little work.

After finally forcing myself out of my truck, I made my way to the front door, hoping like hell they were closed. Sadly, when I pulled on the door, it opened, and I peeked my head inside to see if there was perhaps an armed gunman waiting for me. Seeing no one, I slunk inside.

Despite indoor smoking having been banned for years, there was a haze that permeated the space. Add in the dim lighting and the space would've done a horror movie proud.

"Can I help you?" a voice called from somewhere.

I turned in the general direction it had come from and said, "Uh, yeah, yes, I'm, um, here to meet Charlie. Ricky sent me."

"Oh yeah, he's expecting ya. He's in the back. Just go down

the hall, last door on your right."

"Thanks," I replied to the disembodied voice who was likely directing me toward my death.

As I walked, I made out a bar to my left, and I could see a man moving around behind it. That was probably who'd been speaking to me.

Quickly diverting my attention back toward the hallway, anxiety swirled in my gut. What if they were torturing someone back there? What if they tortured *me* there?

Vee's true crime obsession had clearly gone to my head.

Shuffling down the hall, I stopped in front of the last door. It was closed, and hesitation kept me from reaching for the knob. It wasn't too late for me to leave. I could call Ricky and calmly explain why I couldn't do this kind of stuff. Not that I knew exactly what he was asking me to do. But being an errand boy for the head of an organized crime ring didn't sound like something I was cut out for. Surely Ricky wouldn't want the man married to one niece and dating the other to go to prison, right?

Shit.

That sounded exactly like the type of person anyone with common sense would want behind bars.

I knew doing this for Ricky was stupid. Every cell in my body screamed at me not to get involved. Or *more* involved, as it were. But . . . maybe it was important to show him I could follow through. That once I said I was going to do something, I was as good as my word.

He'd made it clear that this was the way back into the Diaz family's good graces. Didn't I owe it to Vee to try?

With a sudden burst of confidence, I reached out and turned the knob, flinging the door open with the overzealousness of my decision. It swung back sharply, cracking into the wall behind it.

Hadn't these guys ever heard of a doorstop?

The four men, who were all crowded around a small, round table with cards littering the top, all stopped what they were doing to glare at me as I stood in the doorway, wishing I could disappear. Movement caught my eye as I saw one guy reach around to his back and keep his hand there.

Did he have a gun?

"Hi, uh, sorry . . . for the door. I, um, was sent by Ricky?"

Jesus, can I sound any dumber?

"I mean, I was. Sent by Ricky. It wasn't a question even though I made it sound that way. Sorry." Why couldn't I shut up? "He said you had something for me?"

The guys watched me silently for a long moment, made all the more awkward by the fact that I couldn't resist fidgeting.

Finally, one of them jerked his head toward a counter against the far wall. "It's in that bag."

Okay, there were three bags on the counter. I felt like I was participating in a life-or-death version of *The Price is Right*. One was a large plastic bag with *Rack 'Em* written on the front. They probably wouldn't put something in a bag with their logo on it, so I dismissed that one. That left a brown paper lunch bag or a black trash bag.

Since I didn't want to lug a trash bag around, I hoped it was the former. At least a paper bag could be easily concealed.

Pointing at it, I asked, "This one?"

I got a gruff nod in return, and I scooped up the bag and hightailed it back to the door.

"Thanks. Have a good day," I said, because manners seemed especially important under these circumstances.

"Whatever, kid," someone mumbled. I didn't know who since I'd already started making my way down the alley.

I didn't think what I was doing would constitute running, but it was damn close. I probably could've given any speed walker on the planet a run for their money. Ha! I loved accidental puns. But I also loved living, so I didn't slow down until I was safely locked in my car.

Once inside, I exhaled deeply and banged my head against the steering wheel.

There had to be a less stress-inducing way to get a family to like me.

Chapter Twenty-Five

OWEN

My pickup for Ricky was all I'd thought about for a week. When I called him to say I got what he asked for, he told me to hang on to it and that he'd let me know when it was needed. Whatever that cryptic as hell message meant.

After visiting my family and running covert ops for Vee's, the last thing I wanted was to be embroiled in more family drama. But luck wasn't on my side because that was exactly what I was headed for.

"What do you think Aamee's mom will be like?" I asked Vee as we headed toward the restaurant where Mrs. Allen had beckoned us to discuss wedding details. Why I was involved in anything to do with Aamee's and Brody's wedding was beyond me.

Vee looked thoughtful for a second. "Probably a cross between Mengele and Charlize Theron. Pretty but deadly."

"Jesus. That sounds terrifying."

Vee nodded like that had been exactly what she was going for. "She did give rise to Aamee, so . . ."

That was true. From what I'd heard, Aamee had only grown any semblance of a conscience after she'd fallen in love with Brody. Which made sense, since it was kind of hard to be icy when a man who embodied the naïve exuberance of a puppy was constantly around.

"It's weird we were all expected to come to this meeting," Vee said. "I would've faked an illness if I wasn't so curious about it."

"We're definitely going to have a story to tell after it," I agreed.

We pulled up outside the swanky hotel Aamee's mom had chosen for her little get-together. A valet ran up, and I put down my window.

"Is there a parking garage?" I asked.

"Are you staying at the hotel?" he asked.

"No, we're supposed to go to one of the banquet halls."

He nodded as if that made sense to him. That made one of us.

"Valet service is complimentary for anyone with business at the hotel."

"Oh. Okay." I looked over at Vee, who shrugged and unbuckled her seat belt. We climbed out of the car and made our way inside as the valet dealt with my truck.

When we walked in, I immediately saw Drew and tapped on Vee's arm to point him out to her.

"The banquet room is down that hall. It's the only door propped open," he explained as he pointed across the ornate entryway to a hallway. "I was ordered to wait out here and direct people, but almost everyone else is already in there."

"Ordered by who?" I asked.

"The Mother from Hell," he muttered. "Seriously, she

makes Aamee look like a teddy bear."

I gave Vee a wide-eyed look, but her returning one was smug because she'd called it on the ride here.

"Can't wait to meet her," I said dryly.

Drew smirked and replied, "I'll see you in there in a few minutes."

Suddenly, I wished I'd been given an assignment that kept me away from Mrs. Allen longer. Vee and I trooped off in the direction Drew had directed as if we were making our way to the guillotine.

When we found the room, everyone appeared as if they had gathered to hold a funeral rather than to discuss a wedding. Round tables were set up around the space, and Aamee sat at one, her cheek rested on her fist as she appeared to fume. Brody sat beside her, rubbing her back.

Sophia and Taylor were off to the side whispering, and Ransom had his arms crossed and looked almost worried.

And Mrs. Mason sat at a table of her own with papers strewn all over it. She tapped away at her phone, ignoring everyone else in the room.

"What's wrong?" Vee asked as we approached Sophia, Taylor, and Ransom.

Sophia looked over her shoulder at Mrs. Allen before answering. "We've been here ten minutes, and that woman has already asked Aamee if she's put on weight, told Taylor she should cut her hair, and then looked me over and said thank God she hired someone to do our makeup. She's literally Satan in a silk blouse."

I was about to open my mouth to reply when a curt, "Oh, more people arrived."

I spun around to see Mrs. Allen walking toward us as if

she were starving and had just found another soul to devour.

"Hmm," she said as she gave me a once-over. Then she snapped her fingers and said, "You. The one with the muscles."

We all looked at Ransom because who else could she possibly be talking to?

Ransom's eyes widened in alarm. "Me?"

"Yes, you. Get this one on an exercise regime before the big day, will you?" She moved her attention to Vee. "And you—"

"If you're going to say something disparaging, I'd encourage you to refrain," Vee said with the confidence of a woman who was going to absolutely dominate in a courtroom one day. Vee stared back at Mrs. Allen with an unwavering gaze that made heat pool in my stomach.

This was the Vee I'd first met. Despite her small stature, her assertiveness made her a little intimidating. As I'd gotten to know her, she'd softened considerably, and I'd almost forgotten that Veronica Diaz was not one to be trifled with.

I waited for Mrs. Allen to blow a gasket at the way Vee'd spoken to her, but her lips quirked in a barely there smirk.

"You'll do."

"Do what exactly?" Vee asked, but Mrs. Allen ignored her and returned to the table she'd commandeered.

"You're my new hero," Taylor whispered to Vee, who smiled in response.

"Party's here!" we heard Carter yell from behind us as he entered the room, Toby and Drew close behind.

"Keep your voice down," Mrs. Allen scolded. "We don't want the hotel staff to think we're a bunch of riffraff."

Riffraff? Carter mouthed at us.

I shrugged in response.

Mrs. Allen stood and ran her hands down her black skirt.

"If you'll all take a seat, I'd like to get started. I have more important things to get to this afternoon."

More important things than discussing her daughter's wedding? This woman was a savage.

"If you're so busy, maybe we should just skip . . . whatever this is," Aamee said snarkily.

How did Aamee not know why we were here? Did she and her mom talk at all? Though if I were related to Mrs. Allen, I'd probably try to avoid conversing with her too.

"Nonsense. I'm here now, so let's get through the list."

"List?" Sophia asked.

Mrs. Allen shot a dark look in Sophia's direction—likely not appreciating being interrupted again. Drew put a protective arm around his girlfriend, probably in case Aamee's mom struck. It was a valiant though likely misguided move. Mrs. Allen could probably take them both down with one perfectly manicured hand tied behind her back.

She didn't deign to answer Sophia but rather kept on speaking. "I've taken the liberty of drawing up responsibilities for each of you. As members of the wedding party, I—"

"Members of the wedding party?" Taylor asked, her voice especially loud in the cavernous space. She whirled around to look at Aamee. "You"—she pointed at Aamee—"want me"—she then pointed at herself—"to be one of your bridesmaids?"

Aamee looked confused, her gaze straying to Brody and then back to Taylor.

"Yeah," she said, as if the answer was obvious.

"But," Taylor spluttered to get her thoughts out. "We fight *all* the time."

Aamee shrugged. "So? I fight with everyone. It's my love language."

"You *love* me too?" Taylor cried. She spun toward Ransom. "Have we entered the *Twilight Zone*?"

Aamee's glare was withering, but there was something else in her face. Something vulnerable. "If you don't want to be part of the wedding, there's the door."

Taylor laughed. "Oh, thank God the normal Aamee's still in there. I was worried for a second."

"I'm confused," said Mrs. Allen. "Are you not all friends?"

"No, we are," Taylor assured her.

"We just didn't think Aamee actually liked any of us," Sophia added.

"I didn't say I *liked* you," Aamee muttered.

"That's right," Taylor agreed. "You *love* us."

"I'm rethinking all the life choices that led me to this moment," Aamee said.

"So, wait," Carter interrupted, his mouth full of what appeared to be cookies. "I get to be in the wedding?"

Mrs. Allen looked disgusted. "Against what I would assume was better judgment, it appears that way."

Carter smiled at Brody. "Dude, I'm honored."

Brody smiled widely in return and gave him a thumbs-up.

"What about me?" asked Toby, looking unsure.

"You too," Brody answered.

Toby appeared pleased but schooled his features. "But don't I make the sides uneven? Or does Aamee have other people standing with her?"

"We figured you could stand on Aamee's side so you could walk down the aisle with Carter," Brody explained.

"Why is this the first I'm hearing about a man standing on your side?" Mrs. Allen asked Aamee. "That will look ridiculous."

Aamee took a deep breath as if she had to steel herself for this showdown. "It's not a big deal at all. We want Toby in the wedding, but with him on my side, things will be more balanced. And like Brody said, it'll be nice to have him walk down with Carter since all the other couples will get to walk together."

"Couple? You mean they…?" Mrs. Allen turned an alarming shade of red. "No. Absolutely not. What would people think?"

"What people?" asked Brody.

"My business associates, my friends, our family."

Brody scoffed. "I have no interest in inviting anyone who'd judge my friends for being who they are. If they have a problem, they can stay the hell home."

"*I* have a problem with it," Mrs. Allen said. She turned her attention to Carter and Toby, the latter shrinking under her hard gaze, causing Carter to wrap a protective arm around him. "Look, I'm sure you're both very … nice. But that lifestyle can't be on display—"

"Enough," Aamee said, her voice low and calm, but also chilling.

Mrs. Allen continued as if Aamee hadn't spoken, but Aamee didn't let her get far.

"Enough!" Aamee's hand came down loudly on the table as she stood. "Carter and Toby are my friends. And they will be in my wedding regardless of what you or anyone else thinks. It is *my* wedding after all."

"A wedding I'm paying for," her mom replied, her tone indicating she thought she had Aamee over a barrel.

Aamee stared her mom down for a few seconds before shifting her attention to Brody. "Wanna make a wedding cake to serve to our friends in your parents' backyard?"

He smiled. "Wouldn't be the first time," he joked.

I wished I'd been friends with them when Brody had pretended to be married to Vee and his parents had called their bluff by throwing them a wedding in the backyard. Going through with a sham wedding to save face with his parents was classic Brody.

"But it will be the last," Aamee replied.

Brody stood and wrapped his arms around Aamee's waist, pulling her close. "You never know." At Aamee's arched eyebrow, he continued. "We may want to renew our vows in forty or fifty years."

Aamee smiled widely. "I guess I can make an allowance for that."

The kiss they shared then was something out of a movie, the perfect moment ruined only by the screeching voice of the harpy who'd given birth to Aamee.

"You do this, Aamee, and that will be the end of it. I won't support you in anything you do from here on out, financially or otherwise."

Aamee pulled back and looked serene when she grabbed Brody's hand and led him toward the door, all of us rising to follow.

"Aamee. I mean it."

Her mother's voice stopped her, and Aamee looked back over her shoulder toward her mother. "I hope you do. Have a nice life, Mom."

And with that, we were gone.

VERONICA

"Well, that was ... something," I said as Owen drove us back home.

After the blowup with Aamee's mom, we walked outside and talked for a few minutes, but it was clear Aamee wanted to get somewhere more private to process her emotions. I didn't blame her one bit. Her mom was a nightmare.

Toby had also been quiet and had remained curled into Carter, who kept an arm protectively wrapped around Toby's shoulders.

"I feel really bad for Aamee. I can't even imagine growing up with someone like that," Owen said.

"Me neither. Maybe the wedding stuff made her more crazy than normal." I hoped that was true. It was a better explanation than Aamee's mom always being that cold and ignorant.

"Maybe," Owen replied, but his tone made it clear he doubted it.

I sighed and sank back into my seat. "Would you ever want a wedding? Or would you rather elope?" I asked.

Owen shot me a curious look out of the corner of his eye, as if he was trying to figure out why I'd be asking. "I've never really thought about it. I'd probably be fine with whatever my partner wanted as long as it didn't bankrupt us or turn us into Mrs. Allen."

"Hmm," I answered noncommittally as I stared out the window.

"What about you?" he asked after a moment.

I sighed. "I don't know either. I always pictured myself

having a wedding, but I didn't ever really consider I'd be planning it alone. Seeing Aamee's mom makes me wonder what my mom would've been like if she'd gotten to help me plan my wedding."

Owen didn't say anything, just reached over and grabbed my hand and gave it a squeeze.

"If Aamee and Brody let Mrs. Mason host the wedding in the backyard, it'll be beautiful." I laughed. "I speak from experience."

"Was it hard?" he asked.

I looked at him curiously, not sure what he was asking.

"Pretending to be engaged to Brody and going through the motions of the wedding. Was it hard?"

I thought it over for a second before replying. "Some of it. The dress shopping was by far the worst because not only did I not really need a dress, having Brody's mom there highlighted that my mom never would be. But being accepted into their family so readily was nice. Even if it was all fake, they never treated me like they knew the truth."

"My family accepts you," Owen said quietly.

I smiled at him. "I know."

As I watched the world whip by outside my window, I thought about how similar Owen's and my situations were. I'd faked an engagement to help a friend—and because I'd kind of gotten him into the mess to begin with—and he was faking a marriage with a stranger.

Though, I guessed the marriage was real. It was the feelings that weren't. Nevertheless, Owen wouldn't be my first fiancé, and I wouldn't be his first wife.

But like Aamee had said, hopefully we would be each other's last.

Chapter Twenty-Six

VERONICA

I'd surreptitiously torn the house apart looking for the locket, but to no avail. I'd done most of the looking when Owen wasn't home because I knew he'd ask questions.

Natalia had caught me running around like a lunatic a few times, but when I'd been cagey about why, she'd been willing to let it drop. Maybe helping her through her pregnancy scare had made her overlook her propensity for gossip and respect that I had things I didn't want to talk about.

With nothing else to go on, I returned to the attic to start my search over. Rummaging through the trunk that had nearly decapitated me last time I'd been up here, I found a stack of old photos. I'd ignored them last time since they clearly weren't jewelry, but this time I was more inclined to take advantage of a distraction.

I sat back and leafed through them. Many of them were pictures of random people and places. Very few people ever appeared in more than two photos, and I wondered if Minnie had had any close friends after June and Milton had left her.

Despite the smile on her face in many of the pictures, I couldn't help but think about how lonely she must've been—living alone in this big house for all those years, making memories with people who might have been virtual strangers.

Not that I knew any of that was true. Maybe Minnie had a torrid love affair that lasted decades. Maybe she didn't take many photos herself so she didn't have photographic evidence of all the people she'd been close to.

But, for whatever reason, I didn't think so.

As I shuffled through, I thought about my own life. I'd always made friends easily, but I left them easily too. Not on purpose, but I tended to have relationships of convenience and proximity. Until the Scooby Gang.

Had I been lonely before then?

There was a constant sense of emptiness I'd had ever since I'd lost my mom, and I never thought I'd even begin to fill it. But these last few months, living here with Owen—and even Natalia—having the Scoobies around all the time, had filled me up in a way I hadn't realized I'd needed until it had happened.

It was tough to confront the fact that I was in my mid-twenties and hadn't been truly content before. But even with all the drama we had going on, I was still happy with where I was in life.

And maybe when law school began, I'd try to make some more friends that would stick. Some that would just be mine.

I heard rustling and an "Ow, shit" coming from the entrance to the attic. I looked over the lid of the trunk and saw Natalia's head pop up.

"What are you doing up here?" she asked as she got herself fully into the room.

I shrugged. "Just looking through stuff."

"Not to be insensitive, but why are you so obsessed with a dead woman's stuff? I'm beginning to worry about your sanity."

Had I thought she'd become respectful of my need for privacy? I should've known better.

"I'm not obsessed, I'm . . . just curious about what might be up here. Maybe some of it's valuable." Distracting her with the potential for making money was my best option.

She rolled her eyes. "Fine, keep your secret. It's probably boring anyway."

God, she was the *worst*. "Yup, that's me. Super boring."

"I said your secret was boring, but interpret it as you see fit."

"You're annoying."

She smiled and waggled her eyebrows at me as she sat next to me.

"Why are you sitting down?"

She gave me a dry look. "Have I ever told you how welcoming you've been since I moved here?"

"No."

"Good." She leaned forward and grabbed some papers out of the trunk. "What are we looking for?" I opened my mouth to protest, but she held up a hand to stop me. "I'm not asking *why* we're looking for it. I'm just asking *what* we're looking for. And don't tell me nothing. You've been running around the house like a cracked-out squirrel for a week."

I studied her for a second before capitulating. "A locket."

"Okay. Is that the only description you have of it?"

"Do we need more?"

"Well, yeah. What if we find the wrong one?"

"Considering I haven't been able to find any, I'm not sure that'll be a problem."

"Whatever you say, boss."

"Ooh, I like that. Call me that more often."

She shoved me gently. "I'm not feeding into whatever domination kinks you have."

I laughed, causing her to do the same.

We spent the next hour looking through the attic. When we decided to call it a day, we still hadn't found the locket, but I had found something. Or maybe realized it was more like it.

Despite all we'd been through, Nattie would be a person who stuck if I got out of my own way and let her.

OWEN

When Ricky called and asked me to meet him, I nearly had a heart attack. Last time I'd had to deliver the package to him, but this time he was coming to me. And while I probably should've been thankful I didn't have to drive hours out of my way, it made me nervous that he'd decided this package was worth a visit down here.

He asked me to meet him at a diner that was close to my job. I tried not to dwell on whether Ricky kept such close tabs on me that he knew where and when I worked or if it was just coincidence. But either way, I clocked out from work at three and made it to the diner fifteen minutes later to see Ricky sitting at a table eating a sandwich.

As I approached, I noticed two other men I recognized sitting at a table near Ricky's. They were drinking coffee as they talked, but it was easy to see the way their eyes continuously swept the restaurant if one knew to look for such a thing.

Which I did because this was evidently my life.

When I reached Ricky's table, his face split into a wide grin, and he motioned to the chair across from him.

"Owen. It's good to see you. Have a seat."

I pushed my hand into my jacket pocket where I'd stashed the bag I'd picked up, making sure it was still there. I'd be terrified if it somehow disappeared on my walk over, so I had checked for it every few steps.

It was much too warm for a jacket, but I wasn't sure how else to transport the bag without carrying it around for everyone to see. There was a good chance wearing it had made me seem even more suspicious, but the logical part of my brain kept reminding me that strangers didn't usually give a shit about other strangers. Likely no one even gave me a second thought. I was the only one obsessing.

Ricky pushed his plate away so he could rest his forearms on the table, causing him to lean toward me a bit, his eyes probing.

"So . . . how ya been?"

"Oh, uh, good. I've been good. What about, uh, what about you?"

He smirked in a way that was far from reassuring. "Can't complain." He studied me for a moment before asking, "You got my stuff?"

"Yeah, I have it here." I reached into my pocket, but he stopped me with a raised hand.

"We'll make the exchange later."

Later? I needed to hang out with him until later? I withdrew my hand from my pocket and settled it on my lap.

"You've done well for me. My family is pleased with how you've been willing to show your loyalty."

I cleared my throat. "Does that mean that I can, you know, stop?"

He smiled again. "You don't like helping me?"

Jesus, that question was a minefield. "I like being the guy Vee thinks I am. Doing this, for you, doesn't make me feel like that person." I took a slow, steady breath, hoping honesty was the best policy in this scenario. Truthfully, it wasn't all about Vee. I didn't like being this guy either. But I doubted Ricky gave a crap about my feelings on the matter.

I knew I had things to make up for with Vee's family. And I was willing to do what it took to get there. But I also wanted... whatever this was with Ricky to have an end date. What he did was his business. I just didn't want it to become a permanent part of mine.

He studied me. When he spoke again, he gave no indication that he'd found what he was looking for or not.

"I have one more task for you. But I don't want to discuss it here." He raised a hand, signaling to the server, who came right over. "Check, please."

She nodded and reached into her apron, removing her pad, and ripping his bill off. "You can pay up front."

Ricky nodded, then removed his wallet from his pocket and dropped some money onto the table for a tip. He then held up the bill, and one of his men grabbed it as he passed, going directly to the front to settle it.

It was the most blatant mob shit I'd ever seen, and I looked around to see if anyone else had noticed. No one seemed to.

"This way," Ricky said as he stood and strolled out of the diner, leaving me to follow.

Once outside, a black SUV pulled up, and Ricky opened the back door, gesturing me to get in first. The man who'd paid the bill was close behind, and he climbed into the front seat before the driver pulled away.

Ricky made a *gimme* gesture with his hand, and I withdrew the bag and handed it to him.

"Did you look inside?"

I shook my head no.

He gave me a curious look. "Why not?"

"Plausible deniability," I replied, and he chuckled.

"I like you, Owen. I really do." He dumped the contents of the paper bag, causing an envelope to fall out. He opened it, hummed in satisfaction at whatever was inside, and then sat back to look at me.

"I have one more job for you. You do this, and you're free and clear. I'll support whatever you and Vee decide to do, and I'll make sure the annulment with Natalia goes through."

I wasn't aware that he'd ever considered not letting the annulment go through. The possibility that he'd stand in the way of that made my stomach roil.

"And if I say no?"

Ricky smiled. "Why ask that when we both know you won't?"

"What would I need to do?"

Ricky gave me a searching look before putting his hand into the envelope and withdrawing a baggy that he ripped open, causing something to fall into his palm. He held it out to me. When I extended my hand, he dropped two pills in my palm.

I looked at him with a furrowed brow, my confusion clear.

"There's an associate of mine in prison who needs those. You're going to deliver them."

"Deliver them? To prison?" He couldn't be serious.

"Yes."

Okay, so he was serious. "What do they do?"

Ricky averted his gaze to fiddle with his suit sleeve. "That's none of your concern."

That wasn't suspicious at all.

"How would I even get them to him?" I asked. "They won't let me just walk up and hand him drugs."

Ricky shrugged. "I'll take care of it. Money opens a lot of doors, even cell doors. It'll never be completely without risks, but as long as you play it cool, you should be fine."

"Play it cool?" I gestured at myself. "What about me implies an ability to be cool in a situation like this?"

Ricky leaned toward me, his visage stern. "Look, kid, this is a simple decision. You either want to fix the mess you created, or you want to walk away from our family. Those are the choices. I'm not asking you to slit anyone's throat or put a gun to someone's head. I'm simply asking you to provide a friend of mine with something he needs. Kind of like I'm doing for you."

"This isn't remotely the same. I could get arrested for this. Your helping with the annulment doesn't have any risks for you."

"Owen, in this family, everything has risk. If you can't handle it, then it's time to walk away."

I was on the verge of a panic attack. In what world were these the only two options? Sneaking drugs into a prison or losing the girl of my dreams. How had my life come to this?

"My niece deserves a guy who will do what it takes to be with her. Are you that guy, Owen?"

Christ, this guy could really lay it on thick when he needed to.

I glared at Ricky. "This has to be it. I don't want to be involved in your . . . activities anymore after this."

His answering grin was sharklike. "You have my word."

Pocketing the pills, I wished Ricky's word meant more. But since it was all I had, for now, it would have to be enough.

Chapter Twenty-Seven

VERONICA

From the doorway to the kitchen, I watched Owen move around the room, pulling out a coffee cup, pouring some coffee into the mug, and then wiping his shirt with a napkin when some splashed onto it.

"Shit. No coffee today," he said to himself because he still had no idea I was there.

"Here, let me," I said.

Owen practically jumped at my words but quickly recovered and allowed me to get a wet paper towel and dab it onto the part of his shirt where the coffee had landed.

"What do you have going on today?" I asked.

"What? Nothing. I mean nothing special. Why?"

I glanced up at him. "You're not usually this dressed up."

"Am I dressed up?" He looked down at his outfit—a white and light-blue checkered button-up and fitted chinos.

"I'd say so."

"Oh, you think I should change? Is it too much?"

"Too much for what?"

He was acting strangely, even for Owen.

"Nothing. I just felt like looking nice today, you know? Don't you ever feel like dressing up?"

"Yes," I answered. "But you usually don't."

"Well, I do now. New year, new me." He gave me a quick kiss on my forehead before stooping down to check his hair in the reflection on the microwave.

"It's August."

"Yeah, well ... I'm about to begin my senior year in college and stuff. I just meant new *school* year, new me."

School didn't begin for two weeks, but it probably wouldn't have done any good to point that out.

"You're not like ... going on a date with someone or something, are you?"

He spun around, and I could tell from his expression that not only was he *not* meeting another girl, but that my question had offended him.

"No. God, no. I promise. Besides, it's ten in the morning. Who goes on a date in the morning?"

It was a sound argument, but I was still skeptical. "You're acting weird."

"I always act weird." He sighed heavily and then turned to get a travel mug from the cabinet. More carefully this time, he poured the coffee into it. "Look, I didn't want to say anything in case nothing came of it, but I have some interviews for internships today."

I felt like such an asshole for pressing him. "I'm so sorry. I didn't mean to make you more stressed. You're gonna do great. And if you don't, that's fine too. There are a million internships. You'll find the right one."

"Thanks," he replied. "I guess I better get going. It

wouldn't look good to be late to an interview."

"Yeah, for sure. Go."

He gave me a kiss and then turned toward the door.

"Don't forget your coffee." I grabbed it off the counter and screwed the lid on.

He took it from me and kissed me again, this time a little longer. "What would I do without you?"

"Probably leave the house with coffee stains but no coffee."

He smiled, but it looked like it hadn't fully formed. "I'll see you when I get home."

"Good luck."

"Thank you," he said. "I'm definitely gonna need it."

OWEN

When had I turned into such a lying liar? Internship interviews? Vee would probably have a million questions when I got home—*if* I got home—and I wouldn't be able to answer any of them. It was amazing I'd managed to convince her at all and spoke to how deeply she trusted my word, because I was fairly certain I'd looked at least half-panicked throughout our conversation.

Betraying her trust made my stomach hurt. I really needed to get my shit together because the Owen I'd always been seemed to be slipping away, and I was worried I'd vanish completely if I wasn't careful.

I looked at the entrance to the prison from the driver's seat of my truck and made a silent promise that when this was all over I'd come clean to Vee about everything. Then I tucked the pills inside the cuff of my right sleeve and hoped Ricky wasn't fucking with me when he'd implied he'd paid off the guards to look the other way.

I barely remembered the walk to the building and the procedure of signing in to visit an inmate. I had to hand over my license, and I vaguely remember being wanded or patted down. Or maybe both. It was all a blur that resembled a cross between a bad acid trip and a dream I knew I wouldn't wake up from. At least—I hoped anyway—that I'd never have to do it again. Though I guess there was a chance that if I did, I'd be the one in the orange jumpsuit.

Finally, I made it inside the room where the inmates sat at tables waiting for visitors.

Why didn't Ricky tell me what this guy looks like?

I didn't know the guy's race or hair length. Did he have tattoos in certain places? I spotted a dude with the words *Kill or Be Killed* tattooed on his neck—or rather *he* spotted *me*, and I wondered if it was the universe's way of sending me a message.

Kill or Be Killed grunted at me as I walked past him toward an empty table, and I took a seat in the plastic chair, hoping the guy I was meeting would find me before I needed to find him.

As my leg shook faster than a bodybuilder mixing a protein shake, I tried to glance around discreetly at the neighboring tables. As I was eyeing a small child handing a handmade card to someone I assumed was her father, a large human with tattooed knuckles took a seat across from me, causing me to jolt.

"Your last name Parrish?"

"Um, yeah?"

"Why do you sound so confused? You either know your

last name, or you're stupid."

I couldn't argue with that, so I just nodded and said, more confidently this time, "Yeah. Yeah, I'm him. Are you Big Larry?"

As he glared at me, I noticed a hazy cloud over one of his eyes, which also seemed to drift to the side. It made it difficult to tell where he was focused.

"Nah, I'm Little Larry," he said. "Big Larry's six feet eight and four-fifty."

"Ha." I did find it funny, but the situation wouldn't allow me to show any emotion other than fear. "That's funny."

He didn't reply.

"You're . . . funny," I said, my voice trailing off.

He didn't laugh. "You bring the shit?"

I widened my eyes but tried to fix my face when I realized my expression could come off as chastising. And I definitely did *not* want Big Larry to think I was chastising him.

"Should we be a little more"—I looked around—"careful?"

"Maybe. If so, you should probably stop lookin' around like you got somethin' to hide."

I pressed my lips together, wanting to get all of this over as quickly as possible. "Yeah," I said through my teeth. "How do I give it to you?"

"Yo, why you talking like you a fuckin' ventriloquist dummy or some shit?"

It almost killed me not to tell him it was the ventriloquist whose mouth didn't move, but somehow I managed to restrain myself.

"Can you tell me what these even are? I can't . . . I need to know how much trouble I can get in here."

I couldn't help but cast my eyes toward the guard closest

to us. He caught my gaze for a moment before he turned away toward another inmate across the room.

"You really want me to answer that?"

It only took me a few seconds to decide that I didn't. Better to get this over with.

"Listen," he said. "I can tell this isn't something that comes natural to you, so here's what's gonna happen. That dude over there with forearms the size of your thighs is gonna start shit with the guy next to him. When that happens, the guards'll run over to break it up, separate everyone and shit. They'll hustle out the people visiting them, and then you can give me what you brought." He leaned in closer to me, which caused me to lean in toward him too. "You're only gonna have a couple of seconds, so you can't hesitate."

"Yeah. Okay, yeah. But I thought Ricky bribed the guards or something. Why does there need to be a fight to distract them?"

Big Larry stared at me like I'd just asked him to tell me the square root of four hundred and fifty-eight.

"Guards?" Big Larry laughed loudly, causing the guards to look this way. "Ricky ain't friends with no guards. That's what he told you?" He laughed again.

I couldn't do this, could I? It was one thing when I thought I didn't have much of a chance of getting caught, but now... who knew what my future would look like? This was all so I could be with Vee again, but I couldn't be with her if I were in jail for smuggling drugs into a high-security prison. I didn't picture her as one to maintain a relationship with conjugal visits and handwritten letters.

But before I had any more time to think about it, I heard a commotion next to me. It had begun. Whatever chaos Ricky had choreographed was happening in front of my eyes. The two guys were smacking the shit out of each other, slamming into tables and walls.

Then Big Larry was in my face. "Where are they?"

I was silent. Frozen in the moment and unable to move.

"Where are they?" Big Larry shook me, and I felt like a noodle that had been left in boiling water for ten minutes too long.

More screaming.

Other inmates egging on the fighters.

Guards screaming and grabbing the two men who'd started it.

And before I knew it, I was handing Big Larry the two pills Ricky had given me. At least if the guards searched me I wouldn't have anything. For all they knew, Larry had them all along. Larry clenched his fist hard around the pills and remained seated despite the chaos. He knew better than to get involved or draw any attention to himself.

When the guards finally got everything under control and escorted the two prisoners out of the room, they announced that visiting hours would be over for the day and family and friends would have to come back another time. Several women began crying, and I felt awful knowing I'd indirectly contributed to their sadness.

The room began to grow quieter once the prisoners that Ricky had paid were out of the room. We were left with one other guard and were instructed to remain seated for the time being.

Now that I'd done what I'd come here to do, I wanted to get the hell out of here.

I watched Big Larry as he stared at the fist that held the

pills, and he seemed almost contemplative, which for some reason struck me as an emotion Big Larry probably didn't often experience.

"Listen, I know this was part of Ricky's fucked-up test to see how far you'll go to get a divorce or whatever, but I want you to know that personally this means a hell of a lot to me."

"Um, you're welcome," I said, sounding unsure of what he was really thanking me for. He'd either take them and get high or something, or he'd trade them for some other commodity he needed.

"I been in this place for eighteen years, and I ain't ever gettin' outta here." He opened his hand to rub his thumb over the pills. "Least not alive."

"I'm sorry, what?" I asked quickly, my brain subconsciously grasping the meaning of his words before I realized I'd understood them. "What do those do?"

I needed him to say it. I needed to know that I'd interpreted him correctly. I was so fucking close to getting that annulment and being finished with Ricky's errands, but I drew the line at helping someone commit suicide. I wasn't a murderer, even if the person I helped kill wanted to die.

"Give them back," I said when he didn't answer.

The guards instructed the inmates to stand, and Big Larry did as he was told. He kept his eyes fixed on me but remained quiet. Then slowly, he brought his hand up toward his mouth.

This was it. If I wanted Ricky's help, I needed to help him first. Except I couldn't exchange Big Larry's life for my own. I couldn't let someone take his own life—even if he wanted to— so that I could live mine the way I wanted.

I surprised myself as much as I seemed to surprise Big Larry when I lunged at him, smacking his hand and causing the pills to fly through the air until they landed against a far wall. Had the hit been a moment sooner, his hand wouldn't have been open and the pills would likely have remained there. A moment later and they would've been in his mouth.

Big Larry grabbed a hold of me and yelled, "You're fuckin' nuts, kid," but he only held on to me for a moment before the guard separated us. Big Larry didn't seem to resist, and within seconds, I was being escorted out of the room and out the main doors. Thankfully the guards hadn't seemed to notice the pills when I knocked them out of Big Larry's hand. Otherwise, I doubted they'd be letting me leave.

And as I headed back to my car, I vowed to myself that this would be the one and only time I saw the inside of a prison. I wasn't cut out for any of this, and I wouldn't sacrifice my integrity to help Ricky. And if that meant that he didn't help me, then so be it.

Chapter Twenty-Eight

OWEN

On the ride home, my mind flooded with all the things I'd fucked up during the last month or so, beginning with the marriage and ending with what could have been considered attempted murder.

But it was all the things in between that haunted me the most. I'd almost compromised the core of who I was as a person and a man because Vee's uncle had asked me to. Maybe it was a type of peer pressure—though Ricky wasn't exactly my peer—or maybe it was straight-up blackmail. Semantics didn't matter. What mattered in that moment was that I'd been hiding something from the woman I loved, and if we had any chance of regaining our footing in our rocky relationship, I had to set the record straight.

When I opened the door to the house, I could hear Vee and Natalia talking in the kitchen. They were watching something on Natalia's phone and laughing hysterically. Sadly, I knew I was about to take the smile off Vee's face with what I had to say.

"Hey," I said.

They took a moment to settle down and then turned toward me.

Natalia began walking toward me with her phone. "Owen, you gotta see this. You'll love it."

"Maybe later."

Natalia looked a little disappointed and a bit surprised by my refusal.

"How were the interviews?" Vee asked. I could tell she was hesitant to ask, and I assumed it was because I probably looked like I'd witnessed someone run over my kitten with a tractor. "You're home earlier than I thought you'd be."

"That's because there weren't any interviews."

"What?" She stared hard at me, and without turning to Natalia, she said to her, "Can you give us a few minutes, Nattie?"

"But this looks like it's about to get good."

"Nattie," Vee said, this time more sternly, causing Natalia to leave the kitchen without another word.

"I'm not cheating on you. I didn't have a date or anything like that. I want that to be clear." I sighed heavily and gestured for Vee to take a seat at the kitchen table. Once she was seated, I sat across from her. "I did lie to you, though."

It was probably the last thing she wanted to hear from me, and I imagined it would be about as easy to digest as biting off a piece of an old tire.

"I'm sorry. I wish I could say that today was the first lie I've told you, but it isn't. I also lied about where I was going that day in Virginia when I said I was going to work out with friends in the garage."

Vee remained quiet as I told her everything that had transpired between Ricky and me and the errands I'd run for him. I thought I saw her expression shift from anger to one of empathy. I let myself briefly consider the possibility that Vee might have felt bad for me, though I didn't want to get my hopes up that her anger with me had diminished much.

Once I'd shared everything there was to share—everything I'd kept from her—Vee pressed her lips together and breathed deeply. Then she shook her head and let out a sharp exhale that sounded more frustrated than angry.

"Fucking Ricky," she said, her words slightly muffled as she spoke through gritted teeth.

"This isn't all his fault. I could've said no to any of the things he asked me to do. I *did* say no to giving those pills to Larry, and I'm sure that decision will solidify my spot as an outsider in the Diaz family."

She laughed, but it sounded cold. "Yeah, well, I wouldn't blame you for not wanting to be a part of a family like mine anyway. That's fucking low, even for Ricky."

I reached my hand over to where hers lay on the table and squeezed it gently in mine. I was so relieved that most of her anger seemed to be directed at her uncle and not at me that I wanted to wrap her up in my arms and kiss the hell out of her.

"I wish you would've told me this when he asked you to do the first favor. I could've intervened. I *would've* intervened."

"I should've told you, but I was scared he'd stop the annulment from going through, and that would've fucked with not only my own life but yours and Natalia's. I'm sorry I wasn't completely honest, but I am now. Whatever happens, we'll figure it out. I thought about seeing if another judge would grant the annulment, but at this point it's probably been too long, and we'd have to get an actual divorce." The words poured out of my mouth like they'd been bottled up for way too long. "I know I don't deserve your forgiveness, but I hope you'll give it to me anyway. Eventually."

"I forgive you now," she said quietly.

My eyes lit up. Even though she'd felt bad about what Ricky had done, I figured it would still take her some time to get over my betrayal.

"You do?"

"Yeah," she said. "Because I haven't been honest with you either."

VERONICA

Telling Owen about my interactions with June was a release I didn't know I'd needed. I knew being honest was the right thing to do, but I didn't realize how much keeping something from Owen had been weighing on me until it didn't anymore.

"Can I come in now?" I heard Natalia call from what sounded like around the corner.

"Have you been listening this whole time?"

She appeared seconds later in the kitchen doorway. "You two really need to work on your communication," she said casually. "Ooh, maybe you guys should try that strategy Dr. Patel makes us do. You know the one where someone says something they're upset about and the other person says what they said but in different words so everyone knows everyone's heard."

I couldn't even believe the marriage counselor the judge ordered Owen and Nattie to meet with was having them do exercises that real couples probably had to do. I figured the therapist got paid either way, so the three of them were simply going through the motions to fulfill the court mandate. And also...

"That sounds lame," I told her. "I'm calling Ricky."

I already had my phone out, but when I thought better of it, I asked Owen for his. He handed it over with the reluctance of a parent handing over the car keys to a teenager who'd just gotten their license.

I found Uncle Ricky's number and switched it to the speaker when it began to ring.

He picked up after two rings. "I'm surprised you're calling me after that shit you pulled this morning. You're lucky you're not in prison with Larry." He chuckled loudly at his own joke.

"No, *you're* lucky!" I said. "You're lucky I don't take the first train up there and—"

"Veronica? Why are you..." His voice trailed off as the implications of my call no doubt began to register in his brain. Even a dumbass like Ricky could connect these dots. "Shit. It's not what you think."

"Really?" I said, my voice radiating with skepticism. "So it's not that you sent Owen to kill someone in jail today? Because that pretty much seems like what happened, but if you have a different explanation, I'd love to hear it."

As scary as my uncle could be to others, he'd never so much as raised his voice at me. And I was sure this situation wouldn't be any different. He'd fucked up, not me.

"Jesus Christ," he said with a long sigh. "I didn't send your boyfriend to kill someone."

Owen's eyes widened at me like he was begging me to believe him and not Ricky, but he didn't voice it.

"You're full of shit," I said. "You've been blackmailing Owen into doing your dirty work. Does it even matter to you that it's not only my boyfriend who's in a marriage he wants no part of? Your niece is in one too. You'd think you'd wanna help them out."

"Whoa, whoa, hang on a second. Let me explain."

I couldn't wait to hear this. Ricky could spin some lies, but these would have to be pretty damn convincing.

"So explain."

"Okay, so listen. As Owen will attest to, I didn't have him pick up or transport anything illegal. The box from Virginia only had chocolate in there, right, Owen?"

He'd already told me that when he came clean about Ricky, so that part seemed to be true.

"Yeah, I told her that."

"And the envelope you got from the pool hall had cash in it, which, to my knowledge, isn't illegal."

"That depends," I said.

"Fair enough. But at least admit that the cash itself isn't anything he could've gone to jail for. No way he'd be locked up for that, even if they could prove where the money came from."

"So why even have him do this? Are you just too lazy to order candy online or pick up your own blood money?"

"What is it you guys think I do anyway?" He laughed, which I hadn't been expecting.

"I don't know. Someone who puts out hits on people in prison," I snapped.

"It wasn't a hit," Owen said quietly. "Remember? I said the guy wanted the pills. I think it was more like a euthanasia type of situation."

I cast Owen a look that hopefully told him it was time to stop talking.

"Well, it might've been if Big Larry had some type of ibuprofen allergy."

"What?" all three of us said at the same time. Did he just fucking imply that the pills he'd given Owen to smuggle into a prison had been over-the-counter pain relievers?

Ricky laughed again, more loudly this time. "Your dad owes me two hundred bucks, by the way, because I told him Owen would be too freaked out to look at them."

"Glad you think this is so funny," I said. "But our lives aren't toys for you to play with when you're bored."

"This wasn't a game, Veronica. None of it I did for my own enjoyment. Well," he said, "some of it did end up being pretty funny, but still."

"So what the hell was it if it wasn't a game, then?" This time it was Owen who spoke, and he sounded on the verge of a breakdown. I thought I was mad, but I had nothing on Owen Parrish right now.

"It was a test," Ricky said.

"To what?" Owen shook his head and pulled at his hair as he paced. "See if I'm cut out for this scary-ass gang life? Because you don't need a test to figure that out. I could've told you I'm not. I *did* try to tell you I'm not, but you didn't listen."

"First of all, don't ever refer to my business as a gang again. We are a mostly legal enterprise, and I am a very, very impressive entrepreneur. Show some respect."

I rolled my eyes at Ricky's diatribe. No one was more sensitive than those in organized crime.

"Second, I didn't listen because this was never to see if you could fit in. You fit in just fine that night of my dad's party. It's why Vee got all crazy and broke up with you to begin with. The test was to see how far you would go to get Vee back."

This was so incredibly fucked up. I felt sick to my stomach thinking about all of it. "Well, I guess he failed because he wouldn't slip fake cyanide or whatever to your buddy in jail."

"No," my uncle said. "He wouldn't. Well, technically he did, but that was before he realized they were supposed to kill him. Then Owen knocked them out of Big Larry's hand. Your boyfriend's got some big cojones because Larry didn't get his nickname for nothin'. He's a big fuckin' dude."

"He really is," Owen agreed.

"My point is," Ricky continued, "that you got nothin' to worry about with that one. He loves you and would do anything for you. Anything except compromise who he is."

Owen's face lit up with Ricky's compliments, and I wished that hadn't meant so much to him mainly because I wished I would've been the one to say them first.

"Yeah, I know," I said. "I love him too."

Natalia put her arms around both of us and pulled us in closer to her. "Dr. Patel would be so proud."

"Am I divorced yet?" Owen asked loudly.

"Almost," Ricky said on a laugh. "It's in the works."

Ricky said goodbye and not to hit him too hard next time I saw him, and once I hung up, the three of us collapsed on the couch.

"What should we do now?" I asked, turning toward Owen.

Shrugging, he said, "First I thought we could give June back her necklace."

"You have it?" I asked, feeling my face light up.

"Of course I have it. It's in my top dresser drawer. Minnie had it in a small jewelry box, so I figured it was important to her. I didn't feel right opening it, so I don't know if the pictures are still in there, but I'm guessing they are."

"See," Nattie said, giving my thigh a squeeze. "This is the communication I was talking about. If you would've told him right away, June would already have had her locket back and whatever memories are inside it."

"Thanks, Dr. Phil. I'll try to keep that in mind going forward."

"I think she'll just be happy to have it," Owen said. "She's waited decades. I'm sure a couple more weeks didn't matter."

He kissed the top of my forehead and pulled me in to snuggle against him. "Besides, the best things are usually worth waiting for."

This time when he kissed me, it was more intimate, more special somehow.

I became so lost in the moment I'd forgotten Natalia was even there until she said, "Well, I can tell when I'm not wanted, so I'll see myself out."

She stood, and I heard her footsteps tread lightly across the wood floors toward the stairs. "Guess it's safe to say I won't be getting a locket with both your pictures in it."

There had never been a truer statement. I wanted this man all to myself, and that was how I had him.

Chapter Twenty-Nine

VERONICA

I cast a furtive glance at Inez, who looked like she was picturing dismembering all who'd ever wronged her. She was tossing equipment into cubbies and drawers like the materials had personally offended her. We were cleaning up after most of the kids had been picked up for the day. Robbie had the stragglers outside.

"Something wrong?" I asked, a little afraid she'd rip *my* head off for even asking.

She sighed again. "No."

"Okay," I replied, not wanting to push.

She suddenly stopped what she was doing. "I need to move. The landlord is selling the freaking building to some guy who's going to renovate them and turn them into luxury condos or some shit I'd never be able to afford."

"Oh no. Did you check if he can legally do that?" I hadn't studied property law, especially not in this state, but I could look into it for her if she needed me to.

She shrugged. "We all have month-to-month leases, so he says he can. From what I saw on Google, he only had to give a month's notice, which he's doing. But still, a month doesn't give me much time to find somewhere I can afford."

"That sucks. I'm so sorry."

"Yeah, me too." She sighed again. "It'll be fine, though. I always land on my feet."

She went back to cleaning up, more calmly than before. Or maybe she was more resigned.

I hated this was happening to her. She was such a force—a powerhouse of confidence and assertiveness. It sucked seeing her look defeated.

We finished up quickly, and then she told me I could head out. I offered to stay so she could cut out early, but she said she'd rather keep busy.

I thought about her the whole way home. I'd asked around when she'd told me she was thinking of moving before, so I wasn't sure what else I could do, but the urge to do *something* was strong.

Letting myself into the house, I called out to Owen.

"In here," he yelled from the direction of the kitchen.

I toed off my shoes and headed that direction. He was hunkered over the table with his back to me, so I went up behind him and wrapped my arms around his neck to give him a hug and kiss on the cheek.

His hands came up to grip my forearms. "How was your day?" he asked me.

"Pretty good," I replied. "Inez was bummed out." I relayed the story to him as I sank down on a seat beside him and surveyed the papers all over the table.

"That sucks," he replied.

"Yeah, it does." I gestured at the table. "What's all this?"

He blew out a breath. "Bills. Growing up isn't all it's cracked up to be."

"These are *all* bills?" I asked. There were papers strewn everywhere.

"Not all of them. Some of it's information about the house I needed so I could keep myself on top of things like school taxes and stuff."

I pulled a face that showed how little I envied him. "Is Nattie here?"

"No, she left for work a little while ago. Hey," he said, lighting up. "Nattie seems like she plans to keep her job around here. Maybe she could be roommates with Inez."

"Did Nattie say she planned on moving?" I asked.

"No. I guess I just assumed she would when she wasn't court-ordered to live here."

I reached over and patted his hand. "Sweet summer child. We feed her and give her a roof over her head pretty much for free. So unless you plan to start charging her, which I support you doing by the way, then she isn't going anywhere."

"Eh, it feels weird to start charging her rent now."

"Maybe, but fair is fair," I replied. Then a thought hit me like a lightning bolt. "Owen?"

"Yeah?"

When I didn't answer right away, he looked up at me. Whatever he saw must've made him nervous, even though I was smiling.

I reached out and laid my hand over his.

"You're creeping me out. What were you going to say?" he asked.

My smile widened. "Have you ever thought of becoming a landlord?"

Also by

ELIZABETH HAYLEY

The Love Game:
Never Have You Ever
Truth or Dare You
Two Truths & a Lime
Ready or Not
Let's Not and Say We Did
Tag, We're It
Trivial Pursuits
Duck, Duck, Truce
Forget Me Knot

Misadventures:
Misadventures with My Roommate
Misadventures with a Country Boy
Misadventures in a Threesome
Misadventures with a Twin
Misadventures with a Sexpert

Other Titles:
The One-Night Stand

Love Lessons:
Pieces of Perfect
Picking Up the Pieces
Perfectly Ever After

❤

Sex Snob
(A Love Lessons Novel)

Acknowledgments

We have to start by thanking Meredith Wild for her continuous support. It's an honor to be part of the incredible Waterhouse team.

To our swolemate, Scott, we're not sure what we'd do without you. Thanks for reeling us in when we need it while still allowing us the freedom to express ourselves.

To the rest of the Waterhouse Press team, thank you for all you do for us and for not making us feel like the disasters we are.

To our Padded Roomers, what can we say? You do so much for us, and there's no way we can ever repay you. From the bottom of our hearts, thank you for sacrificing your time to help us spread the word about our books. We love you all dearly.

To our readers, there's no way to accurately thank you for taking a chance on us and for your support. Thank you for letting us share our stories with you.

To our children, who are starting to realize what we do for a living. Guess we couldn't prevent you from learning to read forever. We hope we make you proud.

To our husbands, we know it's not easy. Thanks for hanging in there. We honestly don't deserve you.

To each other, for pushing one another forward when we stall. The ride hasn't been easy, but it's sure as hell been a lot of fun. On to the next.

About

ELIZABETH HAYLEY

Elizabeth Hayley is actually "Elizabeth" and "Hayley," two friends who love reading romance novels to obsessive levels. This mutual love prompted them to put their English degrees to good use by penning their own. The product is *Pieces of Perfect*, their debut novel. They learned a ton about one another through the process, like how they clearly share a brain and have a persistent need to text each other constantly (much to their husbands' chagrin).

They live with their husbands and kids in a Philadelphia suburb. Thankfully, their children are still too young to read their books.

Visit them at AuthorElizabethHayley.com